Luna and the *Butterfly*

TALES OF INNER DISCOVERY

GABRIELLA RUJSZ

BALBOA.PRESS
A DIVISION OF HAY HOUSE

This is a work of fiction. All of the characters, names, incidents, organizations, and dialogue in this novel are either the products of the author's imagination or are used fictitiously.

Balboa Press books may be ordered through booksellers or by contacting:

Balboa Press
A Division of Hay House
1663 Liberty Drive
Bloomington, IN 47403
www.balboapress.co.uk
UK TFN: 0800 0148647 (Toll Free inside the UK)
UK Local: (02) 0369 56325 (+44 20 3695 6325 from outside the UK)

Because of the dynamic nature of the Internet, any web addresses or links contained in this book may have changed since publication and may no longer be valid. The views expressed in this work are solely those of the author and do not necessarily reflect the views of the publisher, and the publisher hereby disclaims any responsibility for them.

The author of this book does not dispense medical advice or prescribe the use of any technique as a form of treatment for physical, emotional, or medical problems without the advice of a physician, either directly or indirectly. The intent of the author is only to offer information of a general nature to help you in your quest for emotional and spiritual well-being. In the event you use any of the information in this book for yourself, which is your constitutional right, the author and the publisher assume no responsibility for your actions.

Interior Image Credit: Andrea Marton

Print information available on the last page.

ISBN: 979-8-7652-1527-2 (sc)
ISBN: 979-8-7652-1526-5 (e)

Library of Congress Control Number: 2025912093

Balboa Press rev. date: 06/23/2025

I recommend the storybook to my niece Zsofi, an angel who landed on Earth. With this book, I send her a message to believe and trust in herself, in the boundless power of her dreams, and in the unyielding force of love. It's a reminder that she can achieve anything her heart desires.

But this storybook is not just for her; it's for everyone, young and old. It's a call to notice the joys and miracles that life presents us with each day. It's a gentle nudge to look beyond the ordinary and embrace the extraordinary moments that make life truly magical. May this book serve as a beacon of hope, a source of inspiration, and a treasure trove of wisdom and love to all who turn its pages.

Contents

Prologue

In a world not so different from our own, in a place where dreams and reality dance together, there lived Luna and Iris. Their adventures were like whispers carried by the wind that touched the hearts of many, both young and old. These stories are not just about Luna and Iris—they are about you, me, and everyone who dares to dream.

In the quiet moments when the world sleeps, Luna and Iris embark on journeys of the heart, revealing the magic hidden within each of us. As you turn the pages, let your imagination soar, for these are not mere stories, they are the threads that weave the tapestry of our lives. These tales invite you to discover the beauty within, embrace the power of love, and find the miracles that reside in the simplest of moments.

So take a deep breath, dear reader, and let Luna and Iris guide you on a wondrous adventure. In these stories, you may just find the key to unlocking the door to inner discovery.

1
The Courage to Explore

Luna and the butterfly venture into the Enchanted Forest. Through her encounters with forest creatures, Luna learns the value of facing fears and the importance of inner courage.

Once upon a time, in a world of dreams and possibilities, there lived a curious and adventurous cat named Luna. Luna was not an ordinary cat—she had a heart that yearned for exploration and a spirit that longed for new experiences.

Luna's closest friend was a graceful butterfly named Iris. Iris had vibrant wings that shimmered with the colors of the rainbow, and she had a wisdom that came from years of soaring through the skies. Luna and Iris were inseparable, a team bound by friendship and the shared desire for discovery.

One day, Luna's eyes were drawn to a mysterious forest on the horizon. The forest was said to be enchanted, a place where fears took shape and courage was put to the test. Luna's heart raced with excitement as she turned to Iris and said, "I want to explore that forest, Iris, but I'm afraid."

Iris landed gently on Luna's nose and whispered, "Fear is a part of every adventure, Luna. It's what you do in the face of fear that defines your courage."

Summoning her courage, Luna embarked on their journey toward the Enchanted Forest with Iris by her side. As they entered the forest's threshold, Luna felt a shiver down her spine. Trees whispered secrets, and shadows danced with their own stories. Luna's imagination painted creatures from her deepest fears, yet Iris reminded her that they were just that—creations of her mind.

They came across a creek spanned by a narrow bridge. Luna's heart raced again, this time at the thought of crossing the bridge. "I can't do it," Luna said, her voice trembling.

Iris fluttered around her, her wings leaving trails of light. "Remember, Luna, courage isn't the absence of fear; it's taking a step forward despite it."

Taking a deep breath, Luna gingerly stepped onto the bridge. Her paws felt unsteady at first, but with each step, her confidence grew. She reached the other side, and her heart filled with a newfound courage.

As Luna and Iris ventured deeper into the forest, they encountered creatures that seemed terrifying, but their true natures were revealed as Luna looked beyond appearances. A snarling beast turned out to be a playful squirrel, and the towering figure was nothing more than a gentle giant.

In the heart of the Enchanted Forest, Luna looked into a mirror that reflected her own fears back at her. The mirror showed Luna as she appeared in her moments of self-doubt: small and vulnerable. But then, Luna looked to Iris, whose reflection beside her shone with strength and guidance. Luna realized that just as Iris had stood by her, her courage was always within her.

With newfound determination, Luna touched the mirror's surface, causing it to ripple like water. Her reflection transformed, showing Luna as a brave explorer with Iris by her side.

As they left the Enchanted Forest behind, Luna looked back one last time. The forest that had once seemed ominous now held a sense of accomplishment and growth. Luna understood that the journey had been more than just a physical exploration; it was a journey within herself.

Paw in wing, Luna and Iris returned to their world, ready to face whatever challenges lay ahead. Luna had discovered that courage does not mean the absence of fear but the willingness to confront fear and move forward anyway. As long as Luna had Iris and the courage within herself, there was no adventure too big or fear too daunting.

2

The Rainbow Bridge

Luna and Iris discover a magical bridge that connects different worlds. As they interact with creatures from diverse lands, they learn about empathy, understanding, and the beauty of different perspectives.

In the Land of Dreams, where colors danced on the wind and laughter echoed through the meadows, Luna, the adventurous cat, and Iris, the wise butterfly, found themselves on a new adventure. This time, they had heard whispers of a magical bridge that arched across the sky, connecting lands of wonder and diversity.

Luna's eyes sparkled with curiosity as she gazed at the horizon. "Iris, do you think we can find the Rainbow Bridge?" she asked.

Iris, with her wings aglow, replied, "Of course, Luna. We'll uncover the beauty that lies beyond with determination and open hearts."

With that, Luna and Iris set forth on their journey. As they walked through golden fields and crossed babbling brooks, they encountered creatures of all shapes, sizes, and colors. Everyone greeted them warmly, sharing stories of their lands and teaching Luna and Iris about the richness of differences.

One day, they reached a hill, and there it was—the Rainbow Bridge, its arch shimmering with the hues of a thousand sunsets. But the bridge looked delicate, and a swirl of mist blocked their path.

Luna hesitated, remembering their earlier adventures. "What if we disturb the balance of the bridge?" she pondered.

Iris landed on Luna's shoulder. "This mist represents uncertainty, Luna. It's a challenge we must embrace."

With Iris's words in mind, Luna took a step forward, and the mist parted like a curtain, revealing a bridge glowing with ethereal light. Luna and Iris felt a tingle of energy as if they were entering a new realm as they crossed the bridge.

On the other side, they were greeted by a land that shifted like a kaleidoscope. Trees bore leaves of silver and gold, and rivers sparkled like gems. But what captivated Luna and Iris most were the creatures there who were a patchwork of patterns and colors.

A giggling creature with wings like a dragonfly flew up to them. "Welcome to the Land of Many Hues! I'm Prism, and our differences are celebrated here," it said.

Prism introduced Luna and Iris to the inhabitants of the land, each with its own unique story. They learned how unity thrived when everyone's voice was heard and how understanding blossomed from seeing the world through different eyes.

As Luna and Iris spent days in the Land of Many Hues, they couldn't help but notice the bridge shining brighter than ever. It was a reflection of the unity and harmony they witnessed.

But just as Luna and Iris felt at home, it was time to return. As they crossed the bridge back to their world, they knew they had taken with them the lessons of unity and diversity.

With hearts full of gratitude, they bid farewell to Prism and the Land of Many Hues. Luna looked at Iris and said, "We may be different, Iris, but together, we're a masterpiece."

Iris smiled, her wings casting a rainbow glow. “Indeed, Luna. Just like the colors of the bridge, our world is beautiful because of its diversity.”

And so, Luna and Iris returned to their realm, carrying the vibrant lessons of the Rainbow Bridge. They understood that unity wasn’t about being the same, but about embracing differences and weaving them together into a tapestry of shared dreams.

3

The Song of Dreams

Luna and Iris meet a sad unicorn who has lost its way. Through their shared experiences, they explore the power of dreams, imagination, and the role of hope in overcoming challenges.

In a land where moonbeams waltzed and stars sang lullabies, Luna, the adventurous cat, and Iris, the wise butterfly, found themselves immersed in a world of magic and dreams. Their journey led them to the heart of the Dreamer's Meadow, a place where hopes and aspirations sprouted like wildflowers.

Luna's eyes widened in wonder as she saw the meadow stretch before her, each flower a vibrant hue of dreams waiting to be woven into stories. "Iris, can you hear it? The whisper of dreams in the wind?" Luna asked.

Iris, her wings fluttering like a melody, smiled. "Indeed, Luna. Dreams are the threads that connect hearts and paint the canvas of our souls."

As Luna and Iris wandered through the meadow, they encountered a unicorn with a melancholy gaze. "I am Dreamer, the keeper of unspoken dreams," it said. "My song has faded, and I fear I've forgotten how to dream."

Luna's heart swelled with empathy, and Iris gently landed on Dreamer's horn. "Don't worry, Dreamer. We'll help you find your song again," Luna reassured.

With those words, Luna and Iris embarked on a quest to restore Dreamer's song. They journeyed to the Dreamer's Lake, where ripples held reflections of hopes and wishes. Luna dipped her paw into the water, and the ripples transformed into dancing notes.

Following the notes, Luna, Iris, and Dreamer journeyed to the Dreamer's Cave, a place of deep introspection. They discovered a constellation of crystals, each representing a fragment of Dreamer's song. Luna carefully rearranged the crystals, and a soft melody began to play.

As the notes filled the cave, Luna and Iris felt a warmth envelop them. Dreamer's eyes sparkled, and a tear slid down its cheek. "The song of dreams lives within us," Dreamer whispered.

Luna, Iris, and Dreamer returned to the meadow with their hearts now attuned to the rhythm of dreams. Dreamer closed its eyes, and from its heart, a song blossomed, weaving dreams into a symphony that touched every corner of the land.

Under the moonlit sky, Luna and Iris danced to the song of dreams, each step a promise of boundless possibilities. The meadow transformed into a tapestry of colors, with dreams taking flight like fireflies.

As the song faded, Dreamer looked at Luna and Iris with gratitude. "You've reminded me that dreams are the echoes of our hearts, the melody of our souls," it said.

With a heartwarming smile, Luna turned to Iris. "Dreams are like stars, Iris. Even when they seem distant, they guide us."

Iris nodded, her wings aglow. "And the most beautiful songs are those woven from the threads of dreams."

And so Luna, Iris, and Dreamer stood in the Dreamer's Meadow, united by the song of dreams. With every wish whispered to the night and every aspiration nurtured, the meadow thrived, a testament to the power of dreams and the harmony of hearts.

4

The Garden of Kindness

Luna and Iris come across a garden. By nurturing the garden and helping it flourish, they learn about the significance of kindness, compassion, and the impact of their actions on the world around them.

In a land where compassion blossomed like flowers and kindness was the air they breathed, Luna, the adventurous cat, and Iris, the wise butterfly, found themselves on a path that led to a garden the likes of which they had never seen before. It was the Garden of Kindness, a place where every act of compassion grew into vibrant blooms.

Luna's eyes widened with wonder as they entered the garden. Flowers of all sizes and colors greeted them, their petals shimmering with a gentle glow. "Iris, can you feel it? The warmth in the air?" Luna marveled.

Iris, her wings brushing against the petals, smiled. "Indeed, Luna. This garden flourishes because of the kindness sown by good deeds."

As Luna and Iris strolled through the garden, they noticed a tree adorned with lanterns. Each lantern bore a name, and a soft light emanated from within. Luna's curiosity piqued, and she asked a nearby bird about the lanterns.

"I am Memory," the bird chirped. "Each lantern represents a kind act, a moment of compassion. Every name holds a story of love."

Luna and Iris knew they had to contribute to this garden of kindness. They spent their days listening to the stories of the creatures they encountered, offering a helping paw or a listening ear. Each act of kindness added a new lantern to the tree, casting a warm glow across the garden.

One day, they met a squirrel who had lost its way. Luna gently guided it back to its nest while Iris shared stories of strength and resilience. The squirrel's eyes brightened, and a new lantern appeared on the tree.

But Luna noticed a patch of land that seemed barren, void of flowers. "Iris, why is this spot empty?" Luna asked with concern.

Iris explained, "This is the Patch of Forgotten Kindness. Sometimes kind acts are forgotten, lost to time. But we can help them bloom again."

Determined to bring life to the barren patch, Luna and Iris worked tirelessly. They spoke to creatures about acts of kindness they had witnessed long ago and shared stories of compassion. Flowers slowly began to sprout, and the Patch of Forgotten Kindness turned into a tapestry of colors.

As the garden flourished, Luna and Iris learned that every act of kindness, no matter how small, had the power to create ripples of love. They understood that just as flowers bloomed in response to sunlight, hearts bloomed in response to kindness.

One evening, Luna and Iris sat under the lantern-lit tree, its branches swaying gently. Luna looked at the lanterns, each representing a story of compassion. "Iris, this garden is a reminder that kindness is a gift we can give every day."

Iris nodded, her wings casting a soft light. "And in the tapestry of life, kindness threads our hearts together."

As Luna and Iris left the Garden of Kindness, they carried its warmth within them. They knew that kindness was a garden that flourished not just in flowers but in the connections formed between souls.

Luna and Iris spread seeds of kindness wherever they went as they continued their journey. They understood that even in the darkest moments, a single act of compassion could be the light that led others out of the shadows.

5
The Puzzle of Patience

Luna and Iris encounter a wise old turtle who teaches them about the value of patience and perseverance. They solve puzzles and overcome obstacles, all while learning that good things take time.

In a world where time flows like a river and each moment held a secret, Luna, the adventurous cat, and Iris, the wise butterfly, found themselves in a tranquil garden known as the Garden of Reflection. This garden was said to hold the answer to a puzzle that had intrigued them for a while: the Puzzle of Patience.

Luna looked around, captivated by the beauty of the garden. A gentle breeze rustled and stirred the leaves, and the sunlight created patterns on the ground. "Iris, do you think we can solve this puzzle?" Luna asked, her eyes reflecting determination.

Iris landed softly on Luna's ear. "Patience is like a puzzle, Luna. Each piece connects to form a picture of understanding."

As they wandered through the garden, Luna and Iris came across an elderly turtle named Sage. Sage had a twinkle in its eyes that held a treasure trove of wisdom. "Welcome, travelers. You seek the Puzzle of Patience, do you not?" Sage inquired.

Luna nodded eagerly. "Yes, Sage. We wish to understand the art of patience."

Sage smiled and gestured toward a mosaic at the center of the garden. "This mosaic holds the key to the puzzle. Each piece represents a moment of patience."

Luna and Iris observed the mosaic, each tile depicting scenes of waiting, growth, and transformation. Some tiles showed blooming flowers, and others showed rainbows after a storm. Luna pondered, "How do we piece together this puzzle?"

Sage chuckled softly. "It's not about rushing. It's about embracing each piece as it comes. Take your time, and let the puzzle reveal itself."

With Sage's advice in mind, Luna and Iris decided to embark on a journey of patience. They spent days observing the garden's subtle changes—from the unfurling of petals to the slow dance of shadows. They even helped a young bird build its nest, learning that patience was an act of nurturing.

As the days turned into weeks, Luna and Iris noticed something remarkable. The more they focused on the present, the more they understood the intricate threads of patience that connected moments. They realized that patience wasn't merely waiting; it was appreciating the beauty of each step.

One evening, they returned to the mosaic, and Luna pointed at a section of the mosaic. "I see it now, Iris. Each piece of patience is a brushstroke on the canvas of life."

Iris smiled, her wings shimmering. "And just as a puzzle reveals a picture when completed, patience unveils the art of understanding."

With newfound insight, Luna and Iris gently rearranged the mosaic pieces in their minds. As they did, the mosaic seemed to shift, revealing a breathtaking scene—a garden in full bloom, illuminated by the soft glow of twilight.

Sage approached them, nodding approvingly. "You've solved the Puzzle of Patience, my friends. The garden you see is a reflection of your journey."

Luna gazed at the garden, and her heart filled with tranquility. "Patience isn't just about waiting. It's about living each moment with appreciation."

Iris added, "And within each moment, we find the pieces that shape our path."

As Luna and Iris left the Garden of Reflection, they knew that patience wasn't a puzzle to be solved once and forgotten. To embrace it was something to be practiced every day. They understood that the journey itself was the canvas and patience was the artist's brush crafting a masterpiece of wisdom and serenity.

6

The Dance of Change

Luna and Iris witness the changing seasons in a magical land. Through this experience, they explore the concepts of impermanence, adaptability, and the beauty of embracing change.

In a realm where time flowed like a melody and seasons whispered secrets, Luna, the adventurous cat, and Iris, the wise butterfly, found themselves in a forest bathed in golden sunlight. This forest was known as the Forest of Transformation, a place where change was celebrated as a dance of growth.

Luna's eyes sparkled with curiosity as they entered the forest. Leaves rustled underfoot, and the air carried the fragrance of blooming flowers. "Iris, do you feel it? The energy of change?" Luna asked.

Iris landed softly on Luna's nose. "Indeed, Luna. Change is like a dance, a rhythm of life's evolution."

As they went and wandered deeper into the forest, Luna and Iris encountered an old oak tree with branches that seemed to reach for the sky. The tree spoke with a voice as soothing as a gentle breeze. "Welcome, travelers. You seek the Dance of Change, do you not?" the tree inquired.

Luna nodded eagerly. "Yes, dear tree. We wish to understand the art of embracing change."

The oak tree smiled, and its leaves rustled like a melody. "Change is a dance, my friends. Each step leads to transformation."

Luna and Iris observed the forest around them, noticing how the leaves changed colors, the flowers bloomed, and the creatures adapted to new seasons. "How do we learn this dance, tree?" Luna asked.

The tree responded, "Observe the world around you. Every element of nature carries the wisdom of change. Embrace each season as a new movement in the dance."

With the tree's guidance, Luna and Iris embarked on a journey of observation and discovery. They watched as caterpillars transformed into butterflies and as rivers carved new paths through the land. They listened to the stories of migrating birds and learned that change was both a challenge and an opportunity.

As the seasons shifted, Luna and Iris began to notice changes within themselves. Luna's fur thickened in winter, and Iris's wings shimmered in the sunlight. They realized that change is a reflection of growth, a witness to life's eternal evolution.

One day, they encountered a sprightly squirrel gathering acorns. Luna admired its energy and asked, "Squirrel, how do you embrace change?"

The squirrel paused and looked at Luna with twinkling eyes. "Change is like a dance, friend. Each shift in life's rhythm is a chance to learn a new step."

With each interaction, Luna and Iris learned to appreciate change as a beautiful and natural part of life. They understood that just as a dance had its ups and downs, change brought its challenges and rewards.

One evening, they returned to the oak tree, its branches swaying gently in the breeze. "Dear tree, we've learned the Dance of Change," Luna announced.

The tree nodded approvingly. "Change is not to be feared, but to be embraced as a partner in life's dance."

Luna and Iris took a step forward, their hearts filled with gratitude. "Change is a journey of growth, and with every step, we become more of who we are," Luna said.

Iris added, "And as the dance continues, we find beauty in the evolving rhythm of life."

As Luna and Iris left the Forest of Transformation, they knew that change was a melody that echoed in every heart. They understood that just as the seasons turned, they too would continue to grow, evolve, and dance to the rhythm of change.

7

The Echoing Whispers

Luna and Iris find themselves in a mystical forest where the trees are said to hold the echoes of forgotten stories. As Luna listens to the trees, she's transported into the memories of creatures from ages past. Together, Luna and Iris uncover ancient tales, bridging the gap between generations and preserving the wisdom of the past.

In a world where memories were like echoes on the wind and secrets carried on a gentle breeze, Luna, the adventurous cat, and Iris, the wise butterfly, found themselves in the heart of the Whispering Woods. This enchanted forest was known for holding the echoes of stories long forgotten.

Luna gazed around, her eyes wide with wonder as she listened to the soft rustling of leaves. "Iris, can you hear that? It's as if the forest is whispering to us."

Iris landed on Luna's paw with a smile. "Indeed, Luna. Every tree holds memories, and the wind carries them to those who listen."

As they explored deeper into the Whispering Woods, Luna and Iris came across an ancient oak tree. Its branches twisted and turned, resembling the intricate patterns of stories. The tree's voice, like a gentle melody, filled the air. "Greetings, travelers. You seek the Echoing Whispers, do you not?"

Luna nodded eagerly. "Yes, wise tree. We wish to understand the stories that linger in the wind."

The oak tree nodded knowingly. "Stories are like whispers that never fade, and the wind carries them to those who seek them."

Luna and Iris listened closely as the tree began to share tales of forgotten heroes, magical creatures, and moments of bravery. Each story painted vivid pictures in their minds, and Luna felt as if she was living those stories herself.

"How can we uncover more of these echoes, tree?" Luna asked.

The tree answered, "Listen to the rustling leaves, follow the sound of the wind, and let your heart guide you."

Led by the tree, Luna and Iris set off to discover the echoes hidden in the forest. They listened to the wind as it danced through the trees, carried by the whispers of stories long gone.

Along the way, they encountered creatures who shared their own tales of friendship, courage, and love.

As the sun set, Luna and Iris found themselves in a clearing where fireflies began to gather. Luna gazed at them, realizing that each firefly held an echo of a story within its light. She extended her paw, and the fireflies gathered around her, illuminating the night with their stories.

One by one, the fireflies shared their tales of dreams, hopes, and memories. Luna and Iris listened, their hearts filled with a sense of wonder and connection. They understood that stories had the power to bridge generations and connect souls across time.

As the night grew darker, Luna and Iris returned to the ancient oak tree. "We've heard the Echoing Whispers," Luna said with a smile.

The tree's leaves rustled in approval. "Stories are what weave the fabric of existence. They are the threads that connect the past, present, and future."

Luna and Iris felt a deep sense of gratitude for the wisdom they had gained. They knew they carried in their hearts the echoes of the Whispering Woods—stories of love, courage, and the magic of connection.

8

The Lighthouse of Guidance

Luna and Iris arrive on a remote island where a lighthouse stands tall. They meet a lonely lighthouse keeper who guides ships to safety with its light. Luna and Iris help the keeper rekindle the light of friendship and connection, teaching him that the smallest gestures can illuminate someone's life.

In a realm where waves whispered secrets to the shores and stars painted paths across the night sky, Luna, the adventurous cat, and Iris, the wise butterfly, found themselves on a tranquil island known as Starlight Haven. This island was home to the Lighthouse of Guidance, a beacon that illuminated not just the sea but also the paths of lost souls.

Luna gazed at the lighthouse, its light cutting through the darkness like a ray of hope. "Iris, do you see that? It's like a guardian watching over the ocean."

Iris fluttered down to Luna's side. "Indeed, Luna. The lighthouse serves as a guide for those who've lost their way."

As they approached the lighthouse, Luna and Iris saw a figure sitting by the rocky shore. The figure was the lighthouse keeper, his eyes reflecting the melancholy of solitude. Luna approached with empathy. "Greetings, friend. We're Luna and Iris. Is everything alright?"

The lighthouse keeper looked up, his eyes meeting Luna's. "I am Orion, the keeper of the Lighthouse of Guidance. I guide ships to safety, but lately, I've been feeling lost myself."

Luna's heart went out to Orion. "You've been a guardian for others, but who guides you, Orion?"

Orion sighed. "I used to have a companion, a playful dolphin named Aria. We watched over the sea together. But Aria has not returned in weeks, and I fear she's lost."

Luna turned to Iris, a determined look in her eyes. "We'll help you find Aria, Orion. Let's bring her back to you."

With Orion's guidance, Luna and Iris embarked on a journey across the vast ocean. They encountered gentle sea creatures who shared tales of Aria's kindness and laughter. As they dove deeper, Luna felt a pull in her heart, leading them to a hidden cove.

There, they found Aria trapped in a net, her playful spirit dimmed by her confinement. Luna and Iris worked together to free her, and as soon as she was released, Aria's joyful spirit returned. She leaped and danced, creating ripples of happiness on the water's surface.

Luna and Iris guided Aria back to Starlight Haven, where Orion was waiting anxiously. As Aria leaped into Orion's arms, Luna could see the light return to his eyes. "Thank you, Luna and Iris. You've not only saved Aria, but you've also guided my heart back to its true purpose."

Aria and Orion's reunion filled the island with a radiant light, and the lighthouse shone even brighter, symbolizing the power of connection and guidance. Luna understood that being a guide wasn't just about leading others, it was also about allowing oneself to be guided by love and friendship.

As Luna and Iris bid farewell to Orion and Aria, they felt a sense of fulfillment. They knew that they had not only illuminated a path for others but had also lit up the lives of those who needed guidance themselves.

9
The Enchanted Melody

Luna and Iris stumble upon a hidden glade where a magical tree grows. Each leaf on the tree produces a unique melody that carries emotions. Luna and Iris must weave together these melodies to create a harmonious symphony, showcasing the power of unity and the beauty of diverse voices.

In a land where melodies danced on the wind and colors painted stories across the sky, Luna, the adventurous cat, and Iris, the wise butterfly, found themselves in the heart of Melody Grove. This magical place was known for its mystical tree that produced leaves with melodies woven into their veins.

Luna marveled at the tree's branches, each adorned with leaves of varying colors. "Iris, do you hear that? It's like the very air is humming with music."

Iris landed on Luna's shoulder with a smile. "Indeed, Luna. Each leaf holds a unique melody, waiting to be unlocked."

As they approached the tree, Luna reached out to touch a leaf. A soft melody resonated through the air, filling her heart with a sense of wonder. "I've never heard anything quite like this."

The tree's branches rustled gently, and a voice as soft as a lullaby spoke. "Welcome, travelers. I am Melodia, the guardian of the Enchanted Melody Tree. Every leaf carries a story and a melody waiting to be heard."

Luna looked up at the tree. "Tell us, Melodia, how can we unlock these melodies?"

Like the melody itself, Melodia's leaves rustled. "Open your hearts, let your emotions guide you, and the melodies will flow."

With Melodia's guidance, Luna and Iris set out to explore the grove. As they walked among the leaves, they heard laughter, tales of love, and even the whispers of dreams. Luna's heart swelled with emotions as she touched each leaf, unlocking the inherent melodies.

As Luna touched a golden leaf, a cheerful melody filled the air, accompanied by Iris's gentle wings. Luna closed her eyes, letting the music carry her away. In her mind, she saw images of children playing, flowers blooming, and sunsets painting the sky with hues of orange and pink.

As Luna continued to touch leaves, each melody was a different chapter of life's journey. She laughed with the melodies of joy, felt a tear with the melodies of longing, and her heart swelled with the melodies of love.

Iris fluttered down beside Luna. "Isn't it amazing how each melody captures a moment in time?"

Luna nodded, her eyes shimmering with emotion. "These melodies weave the fabric of existence, telling stories of life's beauty and complexity."

As the day turned to dusk, Luna and Iris returned to Melodia. "Thank you for this gift," Luna said, her voice filled with gratitude.

Melodia's branches swayed in a melody of its own. "Remember, the world is a symphony of emotions and experiences. Let your hearts carry these melodies wherever you go."

As Luna and Iris bid farewell to Melody Grove, they carried the melodies with them as a reminder of life's vibrant tapestry. They knew that these melodies were a testament to the power of emotions, the beauty of experiences, and the magic of sharing stories.

10

The Secret Starlight Society

Luna and Iris discover a company of fireflies that create stunning patterns in the night sky. They learn that each firefly represents a story, and they share their own. On this journey, Luna and Iris discover the meaning of dreams and the importance of belonging.

In a realm where stars whispered secrets to the night and moonbeams painted stories across the sky, Luna, the adventurous cat, and Iris, the wise butterfly, found themselves at the edge of Stardust Meadow. This meadow was known for the mystical gatherings of fireflies that formed the Secret Starlight Society.

Luna watched in awe as fireflies of every hue danced in intricate patterns, weaving their light into the night sky. "Iris, this is truly magical. It's like the stars have come down to dance."

Iris fluttered down gracefully, her wings glowing softly. "Indeed, Luna. The fireflies gather here to share stories and create constellations with their light."

As they approached the meadow, Luna and Iris heard soft voices. The fireflies were engaged in animated conversations, each sharing a tale illuminated by their light. In the center of the meadow stood Lumina, the firefly who led the Secret Starlight Society.

Lumina turned toward Luna and Iris, her light flickering in recognition. "Welcome, travelers. We are the Secret Starlight Society, where stories become constellations and dreams are woven into the night."

Luna gazed at Lumina, fascinated by the shimmering patterns the fireflies created. "Tell us, Lumina, how do these stories become constellations?"

Lumina's light brightened as she explained. "Each firefly shares a story close to their heart. We weave these stories into patterns that light up the night sky, forming new constellations that guide wanderers and dreamers."

Luna and Iris were invited to share their own stories. As they did, their words were woven into the luminous tapestry above. The fireflies' light danced in harmony, creating new constellations that told tales of courage, friendship, and the magic of the unknown.

As the night deepened, Luna and Iris joined the fireflies in creating constellations, forming patterns that told stories of far-off lands, epic quests, and timeless love. With each story added, the sky became a canvas of dreams.

Luna watched the starlit sky, her heart full of wonder. "This is incredible, Iris. Every night, people can look up and see the stories we've shared."

Iris nodded in agreement. "Indeed, Luna. It's a reminder that stories, like stars, can guide and inspire even from afar."

As Luna and Iris bid farewell to the Secret Starlight Society, they felt a deep connection to the cosmos. They understood that storytelling is a gift that transcends time and space, bridges hearts, and illuminates the darkness with the light of imagination.

11

The Mirrored Lake

Luna and Iris encounter a serene lake that reflects the deepest desires and fears of those who look into it. When Luna gazes into the lake, she sees her reflection expressing her own hopes and doubts. Iris helps Luna understand that embracing vulnerability is a way to connect with others and heal from within.

In a realm where the moon's reflection painted ripples of dreams on still waters, Luna, the adventurous cat, and Iris, the wise butterfly, found themselves standing before the shimmering Mirrored Lake. This mystical lake was said to reveal the deepest desires and fears of those who gazed into its depths.

Luna stared at the tranquil surface of the lake, its waters reflecting the starlit sky above. "Iris, this lake seems almost alive, like it holds secrets beneath its surface."

Iris fluttered down beside Luna, her wings casting a gentle glow. "Indeed, Luna. The Mirrored Lake is said to reflect the heart's truest desires and fears."

As they approached the lake's edge, Luna hesitated. "I wonder what I would see if I looked into its waters."

Iris encouraged Luna with a smile. "Perhaps you'll discover something new about yourself."

Luna took a deep breath and gazed into the lake. As she did, the waters began to stir, revealing images that seemed to come from within her heart. She saw herself standing on a mountaintop, surrounded by nature's beauty, her heart brimming with contentment and peace.

But then, the scene changed, and Luna saw herself standing in a vast desert, her paws sinking in the sand. A feeling of loneliness and uncertainty washed over her.

Iris landed on Luna's shoulder, her wings brushing against her fur. "What did you see, Luna?"

Luna's eyes shimmered as she looked at Iris. "I saw both my desires and fears, Iris. My desire for serenity and fear of feeling lost."

As Iris gazed into the lake, her reflection danced on the water's surface. She saw herself soaring through the sky, surrounded by the beauty of the world. But then, the reflection shifted, and she saw herself trapped in a cage, her wings clipped.

Luna looked at Iris with concern. "What did the lake show you, Iris?"

Iris's wings fluttered gently. "It showed me my longing for freedom and fear of being confined."

Together, Luna and Iris realized that the Mirrored Lake was not just a reflection of their desires and fears but a reminder that embracing both sides of themselves was the key to growth and understanding.

As the sun began to rise, Luna and Iris watched the lake's surface become clear and still once more. They knew that while desires and fears were a part of every journey, they could choose to navigate their paths with courage and grace.

Before they left, Luna dipped her paw into the lake's waters, sending ripples across the surface. "Thank you, Mirrored Lake, for showing us the reflections of our hearts."

Iris's wings sparkled as she added, "May our journey continue with open hearts and a willingness to explore all that we are."

12

The Whispers of Wishes

Luna and Iris come across a field of dandelions that carry wishes on their seeds. Each seed holds a secret wish, and Luna and Iris embark on a journey to help those wishes come true. Through their adventures, they learn that the act of granting wishes is an act of spreading joy and positivity.

In a realm where fields of dandelions carried the whispered dreams of the heart, Luna, the adventurous cat, and Iris, the wise butterfly, found themselves in the heart of Wishful Meadow. This mystical meadow was known for its dandelions that held secret wishes on their fluffy seeds, waiting to be carried by the wind.

As Luna and Iris strolled through the meadow, they saw dandelions of every size, their white blooms glowing in the sunlight. The air was filled with the gentle hum of wishes waiting to be heard.

Iris landed on a dandelion, her wings casting a soft glow. "Luna, do you hear them? The wishes that yearn to be listened to?"

Luna nodded, her eyes reflecting the beauty of the meadow. "I hear them, Iris. It's as if the meadow itself is whispering secrets."

As Luna and Iris walked, they noticed a dandelion that seemed particularly vibrant. Its seeds shimmered with a faint light. Luna reached out and touched a seed, feeling a rush of warmth and understanding. "This one seems different, Iris. It's as though it's reaching out to us."

Iris nodded in agreement. "Let's listen, Luna. Let the wish reveal itself to us."

The dandelion's seed whispered a wish into Luna's heart—a wish for someone to ease their pain, to be healed and comforted. Luna and Iris exchanged a knowing look, their hearts touched by the wish's sincerity.

Determined to help the wish come true, Luna and Iris set off on a journey to find the source of the wish. They followed the path of the whispering winds, guided by the meadow's magic. Along the way, they encountered creatures in need—animals seeking shelter, plants thirsting for rain, and hearts longing for companionship.

With each act of kindness, the wish's glow grew brighter. Luna and Iris realized that the wishes are interconnected, each whisper carrying the desire for love, healing, and understanding. The more they helped, the more the meadow shimmered with hope.

Finally, Luna and Iris discovered a wounded bird nestled among the branches of a tree. The bird's eyes sparkled with gratitude as Luna freed him and gently placed the dandelion seed beside it. The wish, born from the dandelion's heart, resonated with the bird's need for healing.

As the wind carried the dandelion seed away, Luna watched with a smile. "I hope the wish finds its way."

Iris nodded. "When hearts join in compassion, wishes have a way of finding their path."

In their hearts full of gratitude, Luna and Iris returned to Wishful Meadow, where the dandelions glowed even brighter. The meadow itself seemed to echo with joy, its very essence a testament to the power of connection and empathy.

As they left the meadow, Luna and Iris knew that the whispers of wishes would continue to be heard, carried by the wind to touch the lives of those who needed them most.

13

The Timekeeper's Hourglass

Luna and Iris encounter an ancient owl who guards a mysterious hourglass that controls the passage of time. Luna and Iris travel through different time periods to understand the fabric of time and learn the importance of cherishing the present moment.

In a land where the boundaries of time were fluid, Luna, the adventurous cat, and Iris, the wise butterfly, discovered a hidden grove guarded by an ancient owl. This owl, with feathers as silver as moonlight, was known as the Timekeeper. The grove was home to a magnificent hourglass that held the power to transport its visitors through the tapestries of time.

Luna and Iris approached the grove with a sense of awe. The hourglass was unlike anything they had ever seen, its sands shimmering with the stories of countless moments.

The Timekeeper, perched atop a gnarled branch, looked at them with eyes that seemed to hold the wisdom of ages.

"Greetings, young travelers," the owl hooted in a voice that resonated like a gentle breeze. "If you seek to explore the threads of time, you must first listen to its whispers."

Iris and Luna nodded in understanding, captivated by the promise of the Timekeeper's hourglass. They closed their eyes and let the gentle rustling of leaves and the soft hoots of the owl guide them. When they opened their eyes, they found themselves surrounded by an ancient forest, where the air filled with the calls of long-lost creatures.

They ventured through different eras—when towering dinosaurs roamed, an age of knights and castles, and a futuristic world where technology danced with imagination. With each journey, Luna and Iris learned valuable lessons. Their experiences were a blend of wonder, wisdom, and growth.

In the age of dinosaurs, they discovered the beauty of coexistence and the importance of adaptability. Among knights and castles, they witnessed the power of honor and courage. In the futuristic world, they marveled at the wonders of human creativity while reflecting on the essence of connection that spanned across centuries.

Through their travels, they encountered kindred spirits and shared stories that transcended time's limitations. They saw how love, laughter, and the spirit remained constant, weaving a tapestry that connected every age.

After exploring various time periods, Luna and Iris returned to the present with hearts full of gratitude and insight. The Timekeeper waited for them, his eyes twinkling with ancient knowing. "You have journeyed through time and brought back its wisdom," he hooted. "Remember, time is a tapestry—each moment interwoven with another."

As Luna and Iris bid farewell to the grove, they carried with them the memories of their adventures and the understanding that the present moment was a gift to be cherished. They had glimpsed the stories of the past and the possibilities of the future, but the present was what held the magic of creating their own story.

14

The Symphony of Colors

Luna and Iris visit a valley where colors come to life as enchanting creatures. They witness the harmony of colors dancing together, and Luna learns that even seemingly different elements can create something beautiful when they work in harmony.

One sunny morning, Luna and Iris found themselves at the edge of a mystical valley unlike any other they had ever seen. The moment they set foot in this enchanted place, they were greeted by an explosion of colors that painted the landscape. The valley was home to many magical creatures, each one radiating in a different shade of the rainbow.

As they ventured further into the valley, Luna and Iris encountered a group of winged creatures with feathers that sparkled like sapphires. These were the Azure Skyhawks, the guardians of the valley. The Skyhawks welcomed them with a graceful dance in the sky, leaving colorful trails that hung like ribbons in the air.

The valley's beauty was not just visual; it was musical also. Luna and Iris soon discovered that each creature had a unique song that resonated with its color. The Red Firefinch sang fiery melodies that warmed the heart, while the Indigo Serenade, a majestic serpent, enchanted with its deep, haunting tune.

Luna, curious by nature, approached a group of vividly orange creatures called the Sunflower Sprites. These tiny beings fluttered around her, singing songs of optimism and joy. One of them, named Solara, landed on Luna's shoulder. Solara told Luna about a great event that was to take place—a magical concert at the heart of the valley, where all the creatures would come together to create the Symphony of Colors.

Excitement filled Luna's heart, and she shared the news with Iris. They decided to stay and witness this extraordinary event. Luna was entrusted with a crystal flute, and Iris, with her delicate wings, would add to the chorus of colors with her vibrant fluttering.

As the day turned to evening, Luna and Iris joined the Azure Skyhawks, the Red Firefinch, the Indigo Serenade, the Sunflower Sprites, and many others in the valley's center. The atmosphere buzzed with anticipation. Luna raised her crystal flute, and the Symphony of Colors began.

The melodies and harmonies wove through the air, creating breathtaking patterns of light and sound. Luna played her flute with all her heart while Iris danced with grace and gracefulness. The valley's creatures sang, danced, and filled the air with brilliant hues.

The Symphony of Colors touched their soul. Luna and Iris felt a profound connection with the valley's inhabitants and with each other. In this harmonious moment, they learned that beauty could be found in the diversity of colors and sounds, just as in the variance of life.

Luna and Iris felt a sense of deep fulfillment as the final notes of the symphony faded away. They had been part of something truly magical and learned that the world was richer for its diversity. The valley's vibrant spirit left an indelible mark on their hearts, reminding them that every color, every sound, and every being had its unique place in the grand tapestry of life.

15

The Guardians of Laughter

Luna and Iris encounter a village where laughter has disappeared. They discover the group of beings responsible for the disappearance. Luna and Iris must embark on a mission to help the creatures regain their playful spirit. They will teach them the importance of finding joy in everyday moments.

Once upon a time, in a world of dreams and possibilities, there lived a curious and adventurous cat named Luna. Luna was not an ordinary cat; she had a heart that yearned for exploration and a spirit that longed for new experiences.

One day, in a quaint village nestled between rolling hills and a shimmering river, Luna and Iris found themselves in a place unlike any other. This village was known far and wide as the Village of Eternal Laughter.

As Luna and Iris entered the village, they were greeted by the cheerful laughter of children playing in the streets, adults sharing jokes and stories, and even the animals seemed to be chuckling. It was as if laughter filled the very air they breathed.

Curious, Luna and Iris approached a group of children who were rolling down a grassy hill, laughing uncontrollably. One of the children, a girl with twinkling eyes, noticed Luna and Iris and invited them to join in the fun.

Luna hesitated at first, but Iris nudged her playfully, reminding her that laughter was a universal language. Luna and Iris soon found themselves rolling down the hill with the children, their laughter echoing through the village.

The villagers explained to Luna and Iris that their village was protected by the Guardians of Laughter, a group of wise elders who knew the importance of joy in life. These guardians had a secret: they held the village's laughter in a magical bell, which they rang every morning to ensure that laughter filled the day.

But that morning, when the guardians tried to ring the bell, it didn't make a sound. The villagers were puzzled and worried because the laughter was disappearing. Without laughter, the village would lose its magic.

Luna, Iris, and the children decided to help the guardians find the missing laughter. They followed clues that led them to a hidden cave deep in the hills. Inside the cave, they discovered a group of grumpy creatures called the Grumblers who had stolen the laughter because they had forgotten how to laugh themselves.

With Luna's gentle purring and Iris's butterfly-like grace, they showed the Grumblers the joy of laughter. Soon, the cave was filled with the infectious sound of merriment.

The Grumblers returned the stolen laughter, and Luna, Iris and the children brought it back to the village. When the laughter bell rang again, the whole village burst into joyful laughter.

From that day forward, Luna and Iris knew that laughter was a precious treasure, a language that transcended all barriers. They bid farewell to the Village of Eternal Laughter, carrying with them the knowledge that laughter was a magical gift that should be shared with the world.

And so, Luna and Iris continued their adventures, spreading laughter wherever they went, reminding everyone they met that in the heart of joy, there was boundless magic.

16

The Cloud Weaver's Tale

Luna and Iris venture into a village where they meet cloud weavers. They learn weaving the clouds is not just a form of art but a way to share love, hope, and joy with the world; and their creations carry the emotions they add.

Once upon a time, in a land where the sky stretched endlessly, Luna, the adventurous cat, and Iris, the wise butterfly, found themselves in a whimsical village nestled on the slopes of a rolling hill. This village was unique, for it was home to the Cloud Weavers.

The Cloud Weavers were a group of cheerful and talented villagers who held the magical ability to sculpt and shape clouds. Each day, they crafted fluffy wonders in the sky, from soaring dragons to playful dolphins, that amazed and awed the young and old alike.

Luna and Iris were fascinated by the Cloud Weavers' craft. They watched with wonder as the weavers danced upon the hill, their arms reaching towards the heavens and their fingers lightly touching the clouds. With every graceful movement, the clouds transformed into marvelous creatures and breathtaking scenes.

One day, as Luna and Iris explored the village, they came across an elderly Cloud Weaver named Elara. She sat beneath a giant oak tree, her silver hair shimmering like moonlight. Elara beckoned them closer, her eyes twinkling with wisdom.

"Would you like to learn the secret of cloud weaving?" she asked.

Luna and Iris nodded eagerly.

"Cloud weaving is more than just creating shapes in the sky," Elara explained. "It's about infusing the clouds with your feelings and intentions. When you weave a cloud, you share your emotions with the world."

Luna and Iris listened intently, understanding that this was not just a lesson in artistry but also in empathy and connection.

Under Elara's guidance, they embarked on their cloud-weaving journey. Luna's clouds were filled with the warmth of the sun and cast golden rays of happiness upon the village. Iris wove clouds that danced with the colors of the rainbow and spread joy to everyone who gazed upon them.

As the days passed, the entire village marveled at Luna and Iris's cloud creations. People felt their hearts lift as they looked up at the sky. Even on rainy days, Luna and Iris's clouds brought smiles to the faces of young and old.

A traveler passed through the village one day and noticed the extraordinary clouds. Touched by their beauty, he approached Luna and Iris. "Your cloud weaving is truly magical," he said. "May I ask for a cloud of hope to carry on my journey?"

With kind hearts, Luna and Iris crafted a cloud of pure hope. The traveler released it into the sky, and as it soared, it spread a feeling of optimism to all who saw it.

Elara, watching from a distance, smiled at Luna and Iris. "Remember, dear ones, the magic of cloud weaving lies in the hearts it touches."

Luna and Iris nodded, realizing that their newfound skill was not just a form of art but a way to share love, hope, and joy with the world. As they continued to weave clouds, they understood that the beauty of their creations was in the emotions they carried as much as it was in their shape.

And so, in the village where the sky stretched endlessly, Luna and Iris learned to weave clouds that could touch the soul and bring happiness to all who saw them.

17

The Island of Whispers

Luna and Iris stumble upon an island that brings to life the secrets whispered in the wind, and grants the deepest desires hidden within the hearts of those who venture there. They uncover the island's secrets and learn that sometimes it's essential to confront our hidden truths and acknowledge our desires and fears.

Once upon a time, amid their enchanting adventures, Luna and Iris found themselves sailing through the open sea on their small, wooden boat. The day was warm, and the ocean lay before them, sparkling like a sea of diamonds in the sunlight.

As they sailed further from the shore, the horizon became blurred by an unusually thick fog that had descended upon the sea. The mist was so dense that Luna and Iris could hardly see beyond the bow of their boat. The world around them had transformed into a silent, ethereal realm.

Curiosity and a sense of adventure filled their hearts, so they decided to sail further into the mist, guided only by the whispers that drifted through the air. These whispers were unlike any they had ever heard, so soft and gentle, like the sighs of ancient spirits.

The whispers seemed to beckon them in a particular direction, and Luna and Iris followed the ethereal voices. With each passing moment, the mist grew thinner, allowing them to glimpse what lay beyond. And what a sight it was!

As the mist dissipated, they found themselves in the presence of an island unlike any other. The island was a paradise of vibrant colors, with exotic flowers that filled the air with their sweet fragrance. The flora was a living tapestry of every hue imaginable as if the very colors of the world had come to life.

But what truly enchanted them were the creatures that inhabited the island. There were parrots with feathers as brilliant as the rainbow, and these birds spoke in riddles that stirred the imagination. Fireflies illuminated the island with their soft, enchanting glow, and their synchronized dance created intricate patterns in the night sky.

Among the island's residents were squirrels who possessed a remarkable talent—they could sing songs in a language that only they knew. These songs were filled with wisdom, and as Luna and Iris listened, they felt as if they were unlocking the secrets of the universe.

The island's denizens welcomed Luna and Iris with open arms, sharing stories of ancient wisdom and tales of hidden treasures. It was then that they learned the true nature of this mystical place. The island had the extraordinary power to bring to life the secrets whispered in the wind and to grant the deepest desires hidden within the hearts of those who ventured there.

As Luna and Iris spent more time on the island, they began to realize that their hidden truths were slowly coming to life. It was as if the island had the power to unveil their deepest desires and their most profound fears.

With the guidance of their newfound friends, Luna and Iris has learned that sometimes it is essential to confront our hidden truths and acknowledge our desires and fears. By doing so we can truly understand ourselves and the magical world around us.

Eventually, the time came for Luna and Iris to bid farewell to the Island of Whispers. They knew in their hearts that they could return whenever they wished, for the island's secrets were now a part of them, woven into the very fabric of their beings.

As they sailed away from the island, their hearts were filled with wonder and gratitude for the enchanting adventure they had experienced. The whispers of the mystical island continued to echo in their hearts, a reminder that sometimes the most profound discoveries are found within ourselves.

And so, another enchanting chapter in Luna and Iris's adventures came to a close, leaving them forever changed by the whispers of the mystical island and the magical world that surrounded them.

18

The Timeless Clock Tower

Luna and Iris find a clock tower that can stop time. They use this newfound power to explore different moments in history, learning about the past and the consequences of altering time.

Once upon a time, in the mystical land of wonders, Luna and Iris stumbled upon a magnificent clock tower. But this was no ordinary clock tower—it possessed a magical power to stop time.

Curiosity ignited in Luna's eyes as she gazed upon the ancient timepiece. She wondered what would happen if they turned the clock's hands. Would time itself come to a standstill?

Iris, the wise butterfly and Luna's closest friend, nodded with a knowing smile. "It seems we've discovered something truly remarkable, Luna. This clock tower can halt time in its tracks."

Excitement bubbled up in Luna's heart as she realized the potential of this newfound power. With Iris with her, she knew this adventure would be like no other.

With a gentle touch, Luna turned the clock's hands, and just as they suspected, time suddenly stopped around them. The world was still as if caught in a silent breath.

Together Luna and Iris embarked on an incredible journey through history, visiting various moments and eras. They witnessed the grandeur of ancient civilizations, the bravery of heroes, and the beauty of untouched landscapes.

In one instance, they found themselves standing amid an Egyptian pyramid's construction, watching as workers toiled tirelessly to create a monument that would last through the ages.

In another, they observed a serene moment in a medieval castle, where knights and ladies danced under the shimmering light of chandeliers. Luna watched in amazement at the grace of the dancers and the intricate tapestries that adorned the walls.

Yet, with each stop, Iris reminded Luna of the delicate balance of time. "Remember, Luna, while it is a gift to witness these moments, we must not disrupt the flow of time. For every action has consequences."

As they ventured further into the past, they encountered moments of both joy and sorrow. Luna learned that history was not only a series of grand events but also the sum of countless personal stories.

It was in one such moment, a quiet cottage in a distant village, that Luna saw a family sharing a meal, their faces filled with love and laughter. She realized that the beauty of time lay not only in its grandeur but also in the simple, heartfelt moments.

Their journey through time taught Luna the importance of preserving history and learning from the past. She understood that even the smallest actions could ripple through time, shaping the world as they knew it.

Eventually, Luna and Iris returned to the clock tower, ready to release time from its standstill. With a turn of the clock's hands, the world resumed its normal pace, and Luna and Iris continued their adventures with newfound wisdom and a deeper appreciation for the beauty of time.

And so, Luna and Iris left the Timeless Clock Tower behind, their hearts and minds enriched by the lessons they had learned along their extraordinary journey through history.

19

The Starry Messenger

Luna and Iris meet Stella, a unique star that can communicate with those who look at it. Along the way, they learn that every living thing has a unique purpose and role in the cosmic dance of life.

Once upon a time, in a world of dreams and possibilities, there lived a curious and adventurous cat named Luna. Luna was not an ordinary cat—she had a heart that yearned for exploration and a spirit that longed for new experiences.

In a realm where the stars whispered messages into the night, and the cosmos painted stories in the sky, Luna, the adventurous cat, and Iris, the wise butterfly, found themselves gazing up at the vast cosmos one bright and starry night. As they looked up at the sky, they noticed a peculiar messenger among the stars. This celestial being was named Stella, the Starry Messenger.

Stella was a unique star that possessed the ability to communicate with those who looked upon her. With a warm and gentle glow, she whispered messages of hope, inspiration, and dreams to anyone who dared to look up.

Intrigued by this celestial friend, Luna, and Iris decided to embark on a cosmic adventure to meet Stella in person. They discovered that, while Stella was a star, she also had a physical form. She took the shape of a graceful swan with feathers that sparkled like the night sky.

With guidance from Stella, Luna, and Iris set off on a journey through the Milky Way, soaring through the cosmic expanse. Along the way, they encountered other celestial beings, such as shooting stars that granted wishes and galaxies that sang songs of the universe's secrets.

Finally, they reached the center of the galaxy, where Stella waited for them. She welcomed them with a radiant smile and shared her wisdom about the interconnectedness of all things in the cosmos. Stella taught Luna and Iris that every living being, no matter how small, was like a star in the grand tapestry of the universe. Each had a unique purpose and a role to play in the cosmic dance of life.

Luna and Iris felt their hearts expand with a profound sense of wonder and purpose. They realized that they were also messengers of light and love in their own ways.

With this newfound knowledge, they returned to their earthly realm, ready to spread the messages of hope, inspiration, and dreams to all they met.

And from that day forward, every time Luna and Iris gazed up at the night sky, they knew that Stella, the Starry Messenger, was watching over them, guiding them on their journey of discovery and spreading the light of the stars to the world.

20

The Forgotten Songs

Luna and Iris discover an ancient where the trees sing forgotten songs. They help the forest remember its melodies and learn the value of preserving traditions.

Once upon a time, in a faraway forest, Luna and Iris stumbled upon a place unlike any other they had seen. The trees here were ancient, their branches reaching high into the sky, and their bark bore the scars of countless years.

As Luna and Iris ventured deeper into the forest, a soft and enchanting sound filled the air. It was the whispering of leaves and the humming of the wind that created a symphony of nature. Luna was captivated by the beautiful melodies, and she asked Iris, "What is this lovely music?"

Iris, with her deep wisdom, replied, "These are the forgotten songs of the forest, Luna. Each tree has its own melody and a story to tell. But, with time, these songs fell silent, and the forest has forgotten its own music."

Determined to help the forest remember its songs, Luna and Iris began to listen to the trees. They gently touched the bark and listened with their hearts. As they did, the trees responded, sharing their songs with Luna and Iris.

Luna and Iris, with each passing day, learned more songs and sang along with the forest. The melodies were magical, and as they filled the forest once again, something remarkable happened. The animals, the birds, and even the other plants and flowers joined in, adding their voices to the chorus.

As the forest sang, it came to life in a new way. The trees grew taller and stronger, the flowers bloomed brighter, and the animals danced to the rhythm of the songs. Luna and Iris realized that the forest's music wasn't just beautiful. It was essential to its well-being.

With their mission accomplished, Luna and Iris left the forest, knowing they had helped preserve a precious part of nature's soul. As they walked away, the forest's melodies continued to fill the air, a reminder of the beauty that can be found when we listen to the forgotten songs of our hearts.

21

The Symphony of Elements

Luna and Iris explore a land where the elements come to life. They must navigate the challenges posed by earth, water, fire, and air, discovering the balance of nature.

Once upon a time, in a world of dreams and possibilities, there lived a curious and adventurous cat named Luna. Luna was not an ordinary cat—she had a heart that yearned for exploration and a spirit that longed for new experiences.

Luna and Iris were on the verge of another extraordinary adventure. They had arrived at a place unlike any they had seen before, a land where the very elements of the world came to life. The earth, water, fire, and air danced in harmony, creating a symphony of breathtaking beauty.

As they ventured deeper into this magical realm, they felt the earth vibrate beneath their paws. It was as if the ground itself was whispering secrets of ancient times.

Luna paused to listen, and Iris, ever the wise guide, encouraged her.

"Listen closely, Luna," said Iris. "The earth has stories to tell. It remembers the footsteps of those who walked here long ago."

Luna closed her eyes and concentrated on the gentle tremors beneath her. Images of people from the past began to form in her mind. She saw hunters stalking their prey, families sharing stories around a campfire, and children playing beneath the vast canopy of trees. It was a history lesson from the very soil beneath their feet

Next, Luna and Iris came upon a crystal-clear stream, where water flowed with a mesmerizing grace. They dipped their paws into the cool liquid and felt its soothing energy. Iris, with a knowing smile, shared her wisdom.

"Water is the source of life, Luna," Iris said. "It teaches us to adapt and flow like a river to embrace change."

Luna watched as fish darted through the water, their scales shimmering like jewels. She saw the ripples created by stones dropped into the stream and marveled at the interconnectedness of it all. Water's lesson was clear: adapt, flow, and find beauty in change.

Their journey led them to a place where fire danced in vibrant flames, illuminating the night sky. Luna and Iris felt the warmth and energy that radiated from the flames. Iris spoke of fire's lessons.

"Fire is both powerful and delicate," Iris explained. "It reminds us of our inner strength and the importance of balance."

Luna watched as the flames swayed and crackled. She saw how fire could provide comfort and protection but could also destroy if not respected. Fire's lesson was to harness inner strength and maintain a careful balance.

Finally, they ascended to a mountaintop, where the wind whispered the secrets of the skies. Luna felt the breeze rustling through her fur and marveled at the ever-changing patterns it created. Iris shared the wisdom of the air.

"The wind is freedom, Luna," Iris said. "It carries messages, dreams, and the songs of distant lands. Embrace its boundless spirit."

Luna closed her eyes and let the wind envelop her. She heard the melodies of far-off places and felt a sense of interconnectedness with all living beings. The air's lesson was one of freedom, communication, and unity.

Luna and Iris learned valuable lessons from the symphony of elements. They discovered the importance of listening to the earth, adapting like water, finding strength and balance like fire, and embracing the boundless spirit of the wind. With these lessons in their hearts, they continued their journey, knowing that the elements would guide them on their path.

22
The Enchanted Garden

Luna and Iris discover a magical garden filled with unique, talking flowers. Each flower has its own wisdom to share, teaching Luna and Iris valuable lessons about the beauty of diversity and the importance of listening to others.

Once upon a time, in a world where magic lived among the ordinary, Luna and Iris found themselves wandering through a dense forest. The forest was unlike any other, for it held a secret known to very few: the Enchanted Garden.

As Luna, the curious cat, and Iris, the wise butterfly, ventured deeper into the forest, they noticed a soft, gentle hum in the air. It was the sound of flowers talking to one another.

The garden was a dazzling spectacle of colors, but what truly set it apart was that the flowers could speak. Each flower had a distinct voice and personality, much like the people in Luna and Iris's world. These remarkable blooms didn't just communicate with each other; they welcomed Luna and Iris into their vibrant community.

The first flower they encountered was Lily, a graceful white bloom with petals like satin. "Welcome, travelers," she greeted them, her voice as soft as a breeze. "In our garden, diversity is our strength. We may be different, but together, we create harmony."

Iris nodded appreciatively. Luna, in her usual manner, purred with delight.

As they journeyed further, they met Poppy, a fiery red flower who burned with enthusiasm. "Embrace your passions!" Poppy urged. "Life is too short to hold back."

Next was Violet, a shy and gentle flower with petals the color of twilight. "Listen to one another," she whispered. "There's wisdom in silence, too."

One by one, the flowers shared their wisdom with Luna and Iris. They met Roses who taught them about love, Sunflowers who spoke of resilience, and Daisies who celebrated simplicity.

The garden was a symphony of voices, each flower a unique note in the grand composition of life. Luna and Iris learned that diversity wasn't just about appearances; it was about the richness of perspectives and the beauty of different voices coming together.

Finally, they reached the heart of the garden, where a magnificent tree stood. It was the Grand Oak, ancient and wise. Its branches reached out like arms to embrace the entire garden.

"Young travelers," the Grand Oak said, its voice deep and resonant, "remember what you've learned here. The world is a garden of souls, each one unique, each one valuable. Embrace diversity, cherish differences, and listen with an open heart. This is how you'll find true harmony."

Luna and Iris left the Enchanted Garden with hearts full of wonder and newfound wisdom. They carried the voices of the flowers with them, a reminder that the world was a garden of souls, each one valuable in its own way.

And so, they continued their journey, sharing the stories and lessons they'd gathered, knowing that the wisdom of the Enchanted Garden would forever bloom in their hearts.

23

The Guardian of Lost Dreams

Luna and Iris encounter a guardian who watches over forgotten dreams. They help lost dreams find their way back to dreamers and discover the power of imagination.

Once upon a time, in a land of dreams and imagination, Luna, the adventurous cat, and Iris, the wise butterfly, embarked on a magical journey. They found themselves in a place where forgotten dreams resided, a realm known as the Dreamer's Haven.

In the Dreamer's Haven, dreams floated like delicate bubbles, waiting to be recaptured by the dreamers who had let them slip away. Luna and Iris were amazed by the vibrant colors and whimsical shapes of these dreams. Each one told a unique story, held a secret wish, or whispered a long-forgotten promise.

As Luna and Iris explored this ethereal world, they noticed a guardian with shimmering wings adorned in robes woven from moonbeams. The guardian's name was Lysandra, and she was responsible for watching over the lost and forgotten dreams, ensuring they found their way back to the dreamers.

Lysandra greeted Luna and Iris with a warm smile, her eyes twinkling like stars in the night sky. "Welcome, dear travelers," she said. "I am the guardian of lost dreams. I must preserve the dreams left behind and help them return to their rightful owner."

Luna, with her boundless curiosity, couldn't help but ask, "How do dreams end up here, in the Dreamer's Haven?"

Lysandra explained, "Sometimes, when life becomes too busy or when doubts cloud a dreamer's heart, their dreams may escape into the world of forgotten dreams. But these dreams never truly disappear. They linger here, waiting for someone to remember them."

Iris chimed in, "How can we help, Lysandra?"

Lysandra's eyes sparkled with gratitude. "You can help me reunite these dreams with their dreamers. Each dream holds a unique key, a clue to finding its owner. Together, we can decipher these clues and send these dreams back where they belong."

With determination and a sense of wonder, Luna, Iris, and Lysandra set out on their mission. They listened to the soft melodies of music box dreams, followed trails of stardust dreams, and collected colorful puzzle-piece dreams. Each dream they returned filled the Dreamer's Haven with radiant light.

As they worked, Luna and Iris learned the importance of holding onto one's dreams and nurturing them with love and belief. They discovered that dreams, no matter how small or forgotten, had the power to inspire and transform lives.

Finally, after days of searching and reuniting dreams with their dreamers, Luna, Iris, and Lysandra gathered at the heart of the Dreamer's Haven. The once dimly lit world now glowed with the brilliance of fulfilled dreams.

Lysandra thanked Luna and Iris for their help, saying, "You have shown that dreams are precious, and even the lost ones deserve a chance to shine. Never forget the magic of imagination and the power of believing in your dreams."

With smiles on their faces, Luna and Iris bid farewell to Lysandra, their hearts filled with the warmth of the Dreamer's Haven and the knowledge that dreams, once lost, could always be found again.

And so, Luna and Iris left the Dreamer's Haven, continuing their adventures, knowing that every dream they had was a treasure worth protecting and nurturing.

24

The Dream Weaver's Loom

Luna and Iris stumble upon a mystical loom that weaves dreams into reality. Through their adventures, they discover the power of imagination and how dreams can shape one's destiny.

Once upon a time, in a land of dreams and imagination, Luna, the adventurous cat, and Iris, the wise butterfly, embarked on a magical journey. An old, weathered loom was discovered in a quiet corner of the Enchanted Forest. Its wooden frame stood tall, draped in shimmering threads of every color imaginable. The loom's aura radiated a sense of enchantment, beckoning the two friends closer.

"What do you suppose this is, Luna?" Iris fluttered beside the loom, examining its intricate patterns.

Luna, always curious, padded closer and peered at the loom. "I'm not quite sure, Iris. It looks ancient, but I've never seen anything like it before."

As Luna inspected the loom, her paw accidentally brushed against a strand of golden thread. The loom hummed with life, and the forest around them transformed. Trees grew taller, and flowers burst into bloom in an instant.

Luna gasped in wonder. "Iris, look! Our dreams are becoming real."

Indeed, the loom had the power to weave dreams into reality. With every thread they touched, a new adventure unfolded. Luna and Iris found themselves walking through lush meadows, swimming with playful dolphins, and even dancing with fireflies under a moonlit sky.

In one remarkable moment, Luna wished for the ability to fly, and the loom obliged. Her paws lifted from the ground, and she soared into the sky, carried by gossamer wings. Iris joined her, and together they explored the endless blue expanse above.

But they soon realized that the loom's magic extended beyond their dreams. It could shape their reality in unexpected ways. When Luna wished for endless food, the forest became overrun with fruits and nuts, creating a chaotic mess.

"What have we done?" Luna fretted as they watched the animals struggle to find food amidst the abundance.

Iris nodded in agreement. "We must be careful with the loom's power, Luna. Our dreams should bring joy and harmony, not chaos."

Luna understood the importance of their newfound responsibility. They used the threads of the loom with great care to restore the balance of the forest. They wove dreams of cooperation, understanding, and unity among the creatures.

As the threads danced and shimmered, Luna and Iris witnessed the transformation. The animals started sharing the abundance, helping one another find food, and living in harmony. The forest flourished with newfound joy and balance.

With a sigh of relief, Luna and Iris returned to the loom. Luna gently placed a paw on it, and the loom began to rewind the threads. The forest reverted to its original state, peaceful and serene.

"We've learned something important today," Luna said, her eyes filled with wisdom. "Dreams are powerful, but they must be weaved carefully and with consideration for the world around us."

Iris nodded in agreement. "Our dreams can shape our destiny and the world we live in. Let's always remember to dream responsibly."

With their lesson learned, Luna and Iris left the loom behind, knowing they could return whenever they wished. They carried the wisdom of their dream-weaving adventure in their hearts.

25

The Whispering Forest

Luna and Iris explore a forest where the trees communicate through whispers. They learn about the importance of nature's balance and the need to protect our environment.

Once upon a time, Luna and Iris found themselves in the heart of a lush, vibrant forest surrounded by trees they had never seen before. These trees didn't just stand tall and still; they communicated through soft, gentle whispers that filled the air.

Luna, always the curious cat, tilted her head, trying to decipher the mysterious language of the trees. Iris, the wise butterfly, landed on Luna's shoulder, a knowing look in her eyes.

"These trees are trying to tell us something, Luna," she said. "Let's listen."

They closed their eyes and tuned into the forest's whispers. The trees spoke of harmony, balance, and the delicate dance of nature. They shared tales of the animals that called this forest home, from the smallest ants to the mightiest bears. Each had a role to play, and all were interconnected, just like the branches of the trees themselves.

Luna and Iris were fascinated by the wisdom of the Whispering Forest. They ventured deeper, encountering creatures of all kinds. They met a family of deer who taught them about grace and agility. Squirrels showed them the art of preparation and planning for the future, while wise owls revealed the secrets of the night.

As Luna and Iris journeyed through the forest, they noticed something troubling. Some trees were missing leaves, and their branches weakened. The forest's delicate balance was shifting, and the creatures grew anxious.

Iris turned to Luna with a solemn expression. "We must find the cause of this disturbance, Luna. The Whispering Forest is in danger."

Luna nodded and her eyes filled with determination. Together, they searched for answers. Soon, they stumbled upon a river, once clear and sparkling. Now, it flowed murky and polluted.

Luna's heart sank. "The river's pollution is affecting the trees and the animals," she realized.

With Iris guiding her, Luna leaped into action. They rallied the forest's inhabitants, organizing a cleanup effort to restore the river's purity. The creatures worked tirelessly, understanding that their home's health depended on it.

As the last piece of litter was removed, Luna and Iris watched in awe as the river gradually cleared. The Whispering Forest seemed to sigh in relief, the trees' whispers growing stronger and more harmonious.

The forest regained its former glory and preserved its delicate balance. Luna and Iris, with the wisdom they had gained from their forest friends, understood the importance of protecting their environment.

They bid them farewell with gratitude in their hearts. The Whispering Forest gave them a profound understanding of nature's delicate balance.

As they emerged from the forest, Luna and Iris knew they had embarked on another transformative journey. The wisdom they had gained from the Whispering Forest would stay with them forever, a reminder of their responsibility to protect and cherish the natural world.

Back in their familiar garden, Luna and Iris shared their experiences with the others. Their friends listened intently, inspired by the tales of the Whispering Forest. Together, they pledged to take better care of their environment to ensure that their own garden remained a sanctuary of balance and harmony.

And so, Luna and Iris's adventures continued to each tell a lesson, each journey a discovery. The bond between the cat and the butterfly grew stronger with every adventure, a testament to the power of friendship and shared wisdom.

As Luna settled in for her afternoon nap, Iris perched on her shoulder, her wings glistening in the dappled sunlight. They both knew that the world was full of wonders waiting to be explored, and they were ready for whatever came their way.

26

The Song of the Stars

Luna and Iris embark on a journey to a place where stars sing beautiful melodies. They learn about the interconnectedness of the universe and how small actions can create significant ripples in the world.

Once upon a time, in the heart of a tranquil night, Luna and Iris found themselves in a vast meadow, gazing up at a sky strewn with brilliant stars. As they admired the celestial display, they noticed something extraordinary—the stars weren't just shining, they were singing.

Amazed, Luna and Iris followed the enchanting melody, which led them to a clearing in the meadow. In the center of this clearing stood a majestic ancient oak tree, its branches reaching out to the sky, adorned with countless fireflies that themselves twinkled like stars.

Beneath the tree, they found a radiant being known as Celestia, who was the guardian of this mystical place. Celestia's eyes sparkled like the heavens above, and she welcomed Luna and Iris with a serene smile.

"You've come to the home of the Singing Stars," Celestia whispered, her voice as melodic as a gentle breeze. "Each star you see in the sky has its song—a unique vibration that resonates throughout the cosmos. These songs tell stories, offer guidance, and bring harmony to the universe."

Luna and Iris were mesmerized by the idea that every star possessed a song. Celestia continued, "But there's more to this cosmic chorus. Stars also listen to the songs of other stars and create their melodies in response. They harmonize, creating a symphony that binds them together."

Luna, feeling a deep connection to the stars, asked, "What can we learn from the songs of the stars?"

Celestia smiled kindly and replied, "You can learn that even the smallest actions, like a single star's note in the vast symphony of the cosmos has an impact. Each choice you make, each act of kindness or love, send ripples through the universe, affecting everything around you."

With newfound understanding, Luna and Iris returned to their world. They began to appreciate the beauty of small actions, realizing that kindness, compassion, and love were their unique songs in the grand melody of life.

Every night, as Luna and Iris gazed upon the stars, they remembered Celestia's teachings. They felt a profound connection to the universe. They knew that by adding their songs of goodness to the cosmic symphony, they were making the world a more harmonious place.

And so, the journey of Luna and Iris continued, guided by the wisdom of the singing stars and the gentle reminder that even the smallest actions could create beautiful ripples in the world.

27

The Puzzle of Possibilities

Luna and Iris enter a world where puzzles come to life. They discover that life is like a puzzle, and each piece plays a crucial role in shaping the bigger picture.

Once upon a time, in a world of dreams and possibilities, Luna and Iris found themselves in a world unlike any they had ever seen before. Everything around them seemed to be made up of colorful puzzle pieces that floated in the air, forming intricate patterns and structures. It was as if they had stepped into a giant living jigsaw puzzle.

Curious as always, Luna and Iris began to explore this puzzling world. They noticed that each puzzle piece had a unique shape, color, and design. Some parts were small and simple, while others were large and intricate. Luna and Iris quickly realized that these puzzle pieces represented the various options and possibilities in life.

As they wandered deeper into the world of puzzles, Luna and Iris encountered other beings who seemed to be engaged in various activities. One creature was diligently fitting pieces together, creating beautiful pictures and scenes. Another struggled to fit the parts and had moments of frustration. Luna and Iris watched and learned from these creatures, understanding that life could be both challenging and rewarding.

The puzzle world taught Luna and Iris an essential lesson: life is like a giant puzzle, and each choice, experience, and person they encountered was a unique puzzle piece. Every piece played a crucial role in creating the bigger picture of their journey.

In this world, Luna and Iris also discovered that they could rearrange puzzle pieces. With great care and thought, they started to arrange the pieces in different ways to create new patterns and pictures. Some of these arrangements led to exciting adventures, while others brought valuable lessons and insights.

But Luna and Iris soon realized that it was not possible to force all the parts together. Certain pieces had to be in certain places, just as infallible experiences had to happen. They learned the importance of patience and acceptance, understanding that not every puzzle had an immediate solution.

As they continued to explore, Luna and Iris noticed that some of the puzzle pieces were missing, leaving gaps in the overall picture. It reminded them that life wasn't always perfect and that sometimes we have to embrace imperfections and uncertainties.

Luna and Iris grew wiser with each step they took in the puzzle world. They understood that the puzzle of life was vast and complex, filled with countless possibilities. They also learned that the beauty of life lay not only in solving the puzzle but also in enjoying the journey of discovery.

As Luna and Iris left the puzzle world, they carried this newfound wisdom with them. They knew that life would continue to present them with challenges, choices, and opportunities, but they were now better equipped to face them. They learned that life, like a jigsaw puzzle, should be explored, cherished, and appreciated piece by piece.

28

The Mysterious Lighthouse

Luna and Iris come across a lighthouse that guides lost souls. Through their exploration, they learn about the importance of helping others find their way in life.

Once upon a time, in a world of dreams and possibilities, Luna and Iris were strolling along the shoreline when they spotted a lighthouse standing tall against the horizon. Its light, a beacon of hope, cut through the evening mist and danced upon the restless waves. It was unlike any lighthouse they had ever seen.

Intrigued by this mysterious structure, Luna and Iris decided to venture closer. As they approached, they noticed that this lighthouse seemed to be reaching out to lost souls. Its light had an aura of compassion and guidance and emitted a soft, melodic hum.

Luna knocked on the large wooden door of the lighthouse with Iris on her shoulder. It creaked open to reveal a warm and welcoming interior. A guardian spirit awaited them inside, its presence radiating wisdom and kindness.

"Welcome, travelers," the guardian spirit greeted them. "I am the keeper of this lighthouse, and my purpose is to guide lost souls. You see, Luna and Iris, there are many lost souls in the world—people who have lost their way, their purpose, or their hope. They wander in darkness, unable to find the path that leads them to fulfillment and happiness."

Luna and Iris listened intently with empathetic hearts. The guardian spirit continued, "My role is to shine a light on their path, to help them navigate the storms of life and find their way back to the shores of hope and purpose. And I'm here to teach you both the importance of helping others find their way."

Guided by the guardian spirit, Luna and Iris learned to send out their own beacons of light. They realized that small acts of kindness, a listening ear, or a supportive hand could be a guiding light for someone lost in the vast sea of life's challenges.

They spent days at the lighthouse assisting the guardian spirit in its noble task. They would send their light into the night, helping lost souls find their way home. And as they did, they witnessed the transformation in these lost souls; how a little guidance and compassion could rekindle their hope and set them on a new, brighter path.

When Luna and Iris left the mysterious lighthouse, they knew that this experience had changed them. They understood that they, too, could be guiding lights for those in need, helping them find their way through the darkest of nights.

With newfound purpose and a heart filled with compassion, they continued their journey, ready to shine their light on the world. They had learned that sometimes the biggest adventure of all is the journey of helping others find their way in life.

29

The Dancing Shadows

Luna and Iris enter a world where shadows have a life of their own. They discover the beauty in embracing both light and darkness; and how each has a unique role to play.

In a land unknown to most, where sunsets painted the sky in brilliant orange and purple hues, Luna and Iris stumbled upon a world the likes of which they had never seen before. It was a place where shadows danced freely, celebrating their existence.

Luna, always curious, approached the shadows cautiously. They swirled and twirled, forming intricate patterns on the ground. Iris, the ever-wise butterfly, whispered to Luna, "Look how gracefully they move, Luna. Shadows aren't just the absence of light; they are a part of the enchanting dance of life."

As Luna watched the mesmerizing display, she noticed something remarkable. Each shadow was unique, taking on different shapes and sizes, reflecting the objects that cast them. Some were long and slender, while others were short and stout. Some danced gracefully, while others moved with a playful bounce.

Luna couldn't help but ask, "Why are these shadows so different from one another, Iris?"

Iris replied, "Just like people, Luna, each shadow is distinct, shaped by its own experiences. Some may be cast by tall trees, while others by small flowers. Some may have experienced harsh sunlight, while others have danced in the gentle glow of twilight. It's these differences that make them beautiful."

Embracing this newfound wisdom, Luna and Iris decided to join the dance of shadows. Luna's shadow stretched tall and curious, while Iris's shadow fluttered. They danced together, creating a unique silhouette in the twilight.

Luna and Iris realized the profound truth about light and darkness when the sun dipped below the horizon, casting long shadows across the land. Just as shadows complemented the light, the challenges and the difficulties in life complemented the moments of joy and happiness.

They continued to dance, celebrating the harmony of light and dark, knowing that each had a role to play in the beautiful tapestry of existence.

The night sky adorned itself with stars, and Luna pointed to the constellations, saying, "Look, Iris, even the stars are like the shadows in the sky, each one shining with its unique brilliance."

Iris nodded in agreement. "Yes, Luna, just like the shadows on the ground, the stars in the sky remind us that our differences make us shine brighter when we come together."

With this newfound understanding, Luna and Iris left the land of dancing shadows with their hearts filled with wisdom and acceptance. They knew that life's dance was a beautiful, ever-changing rhythm, and they were ready to embrace it with grace and open hearts.

And so, as they ventured forth on their journey, Luna and Iris cherished the memory of the dancing shadows, a reminder that in the intricate tapestry of life, every shadow, every experience and every moment played a vital part in creating a more beautiful and harmonious world.

30

The Library of Whispers

Luna and Iris find a library filled with books that whisper secrets to those who read them. They learn about the power of knowledge, curiosity, and the importance of lifelong learning.

In the heart of a hidden forest, where sunlight filtered through the emerald leaves and dappled the forest floor with its gentle glow, Luna and Iris stumbled upon a library the likes of which they had never seen before. The building seemed to be a part of the forest itself, its walls entwined with vines, its roof covered in moss, and its entrance framed by cascading ivy. But what truly set this library apart were its books.

As they crossed the threshold, the duo were greeted by a soft symphony of whispers. It was as if the very books were speaking to them the secrets contained within their pages, longing to be shared. The library held books on every subject imaginable, from ancient histories to magical spells to tales of far-off lands. Each tome had its own story, eager to be discovered.

The place piqued Luna's curiosity, and she reached for a dusty, leather-bound book that sat on a weathered shelf. But before her fingers could even touch the spine, the book gently floated off the shelf and opened itself. Words appeared upon its pages, shimmering like stars in the night sky. Luna began to read aloud. And as she did, the story came to life before her eyes.

Iris, ever the observant one, watched in awe as the characters and landscapes unfolded in the air around them. It was as if they had stepped into the world of the book, becoming part of its narrative. They laughed with the characters, cried at their sorrows, and marveled at the wonders of far-off realms.

Time seemed to stand still as they explored the library. Book after book revealed its secrets to Luna and Iris, each one teaching them something new about the world and themselves. But it wasn't just knowledge that the library imparted; it was a sense of wonder and endless possibility.

As they continued to read, Luna and Iris noticed something remarkable. The books didn't just contain stories. They also held the collective knowledge of the world. Luna learned about the stars and the galaxies, their distant beauty and mysteries. Iris understood the delicate balance of ecosystems; she delved into the intricate web of the natural world.

But with knowledge came a sense of responsibility. Luna and Iris realized that they were now stewards of this wisdom, entrusted to use it wisely and share it with others. They couldn't keep the secrets of the library to themselves; it had to be shared with the world.

They reluctantly left the library with heavy hearts, knowing that their journey has only just begun. As they ventured back into the forest, the library seemed to fade behind them, its whispers growing fainter. Yet they carried its teachings with them, etched into their hearts.

The library had taught them that knowledge was a gift, but it was also a responsibility. They vowed to use the wisdom they had gained to make the world a better place, to kindle curiosity in others, and pass on the magic of lifelong learning.

And so, Luna and Iris continued their adventures, guided by their curiosity and also by the profound lessons they had learned in the Library of Whispers.

31

The Rainbow Painter's Studio

Luna and Iris visit an artist's studio where rainbows are painted. They discover the magic of creativity and self-expression, as well as the beauty of embracing one's unique colors.

Once upon a time, in a world of dreams and possibilities, there lived a curious and adventurous cat named Luna. Luna was not an ordinary cat—she had a heart that yearned for exploration and a spirit that longed for new experiences.

In the heart of the Enchanted Forest, where the leaves sparkled with dewdrops like a thousand diamonds, Luna and Iris stumbled upon a quaint little cottage. The cottage looked ordinary from the outside, with its thatched roof and colorful garden, but it held a secret that would fill their hearts with wonder.

They were greeted by an explosion of colors as Luna and Iris entered the cottage. Paintings of rainbows in every imaginable shade adorned the walls. An elderly and kind woman with a warm smile stood in the middle of the studio, holding a brush dripping with vibrant colors.

"Welcome, dear travelers," she said, her eyes twinkling like stars. "I am Aurora, the Rainbow Painter."

Luna and Iris couldn't contain their excitement. They watched in awe as Aurora dipped her brush into a pot of golden paint and painted a radiant arc of light across the canvas. The colors danced and swirled, creating a breathtaking rainbow.

"How do you do it?" Luna asked, her eyes wide with wonder.

Aurora chuckled softly. "My dear, every rainbow has a story. I listen to the whispers of the wind, the laughter of the leaves, and the songs of the birds. They tell me the colors their hearts desire, and I paint their dreams."

Aurora then invited Luna and Iris to join her in painting rainbows. Luna chose a palette of gentle pastels, while Iris opted for bold and vibrant hues. They dipped their brushes into pots of paint and let their creativity flow.

As Luna painted, she felt a sense of calm and joy wash over her. She realized that the colors she chose reflected her emotions and thoughts. The pastels represented her peaceful moments, while the brighter colors symbolized her dreams and aspirations.

Iris, on the other hand, embraced her bold and unique colors. She understood that each hue represented a part of her personality and experiences. Just like a rainbow, she was a beautiful blend of different shades, and she embraced every one of them.

Hours turned into moments as they painted together, sharing stories and laughter with Aurora. When they finally finished, Luna and Iris stepped back to admire their work. They had created rainbows that were not just on canvas but in their hearts as well.

Aurora smiled with pride. "Remember, my dear friends, creativity is a gift that allows you to express your true self. Embrace your unique colors and share them with the world."

Luna and Iris bid farewell to the Rainbow Painter and her magical studio with hearts full of gratitude. As they left, they carried with them the knowledge that creativity was a beautiful way to express themselves and connect with the world around them.

And so, their journey continued, each step colored by the vibrant rainbows they had painted and the wisdom they had gained from the enchanting artist Aurora.

32

The Tale of Timeless Friendship

Luna and Iris meet characters who have been friends for centuries. Through their journey, they learn about the enduring power of friendship and how it can withstand the test of time.

Once upon a time, in a land not too far away, Luna and Iris found themselves in a place where time seemed to stand still. They came across two remarkable creatures as they wandered through a serene forest. A wise old owl named Oliver and a gentle deer named Delilah.

Oliver and Delilah were not your ordinary forest inhabitants. They had been the best of friends for centuries, their friendship enduring like the ancient trees that surrounded them. Luna and Iris were intrigued and wanted to learn the secret behind such a timeless friendship.

Oliver, with his wide, knowing eyes, shared their story. "Delilah and I met under this very oak tree," he said, pointing to the massive oak that cast a cooling shade over them. "It was a different time back then, but one thing remained constant: our unwavering trust in each other."

Delilah nodded in agreement. She added, "We've seen countless seasons together, weathered storms, and celebrated the joys of life. Our bond is like the roots of these ancient trees, deep and unbreakable."

As Luna and Iris listened to their story, they realized that the key to a timeless friendship is not just sharing good times but also supporting each other through the challenges that life inevitably brings. Oliver and Delilah had stood by each other in times of need and offered comfort and strength to the other.

The four friends spent the day exploring the forest, their laughter echoing through the woods. They discovered a hidden grove where the trees whispered tales of friendships that blossomed and withered, reminding them of the fragility of relationships.

As the sun began to set, Luna and Iris felt a deep sense of gratitude for this unexpected encounter. They realized that the most precious treasure in life is not measured in riches but in the bonds of friendship that they had nurtured along the way.

Before they departed, Oliver shared some timeless advice: "Remember, my dear friends, friendship is like a tree. It may start as a tiny seed, but with care, trust, and time, it can grow into something strong and beautiful."

Luna and Iris left the enchanted forest with their hearts full of newfound wisdom. They knew that the friendships they cherished would stand the test of time if they nurtured them with love, trust, and unwavering support.

And so, their journey continued, carrying with them the timeless lessons they had learned from Oliver and Delilah about the enduring power of friendship, a bond that could withstand the ages.

33

The Song of the Seasons

Luna and Iris stumble upon a hidden grove where the seasons are exist side by side. They learn about the cyclical nature of life, the beauty of change, and how every season has its own unique magic.

Once upon a time, in a land not so far away, Luna and Iris found themselves on an enchanting journey through a hidden grove. As they stepped deeper into the forest, they noticed something extraordinary: each part of the grove represented a different season.

In the heart of the grove stood a magnificent tree, its branches adorned with vibrant blossoms of spring. The air was filled with the sweet scent of flowers, and Luna and Iris could feel the gentle breeze of spring whispering tales of rebirth and growth.

"Isn't spring wonderful?" Iris exclaimed. "It's a season of new beginnings, where life awakens from its slumber."

Luna nodded in agreement, her eyes sparkling with curiosity. As they continued their exploration, they came upon a serene pond, the water shimmering like liquid silver. Here the warmth of summer enveloped them and the sound of birdsong filled the air.

"Summer is a time of joy and abundance," Luna observed. "It's a season of long days and endless adventures."

Their journey led them to a grove blanketed in fiery hues of red and orange. Here, autumn reigned supreme. The ground was carpeted with fallen leaves, and a gentle rustling filled the air.

"Autumn is a season of change and reflection," Iris mused. "It teaches us the beauty of letting go and embracing transformation."

Finally, Luna and Iris reached a clearing where winter's touch could be felt. The tree branches were covered in a delicate layer of frost and stood tall and bare. The air was sharp and crisp, and the sky was a brilliant shade of blue.

"Winter may seem cold and stark," Luna said, "but it holds a unique kind of magic. It's a season of rest and introspection, where nature finds solace in stillness."

As Luna and Iris continued their journey through the grove, they realized that each season had its special song. The songs harmonized together, creating a symphony of life's cyclical nature. They understood that just as the seasons changed, so did their own lives, and there was beauty in every phase of existence.

Before leaving the grove, Luna and Iris made a promise to embrace the magic of each season, in nature and in themselves. They understood that life was a continuous cycle, and just like the seasons, they would experience growth, joy, change, and stillness.

Luna and Iris left the hidden grove with newfound wisdom and their hearts filled with gratitude for the lessons. As they ventured back into the world, they carried the songs of the seasons with them, a reminder of the beauty of life's ever-turning wheel.

And so, their journey continued as Luna and Iris danced through the seasons of life, embracing each one with open hearts and open minds.

34

The Starlight Voyage

Luna and Iris embark on a journey to the night sky, where they meet constellations that come to life. They learn about the stories behind the stars and how dreams can guide one's path.

Once upon a time, in the tranquil town of Serendipity Springs, Luna, and Iris were out exploring the wonders of the night sky. The town was known for its clear, starry nights, and the duo felt drawn to the twinkling lights above.

One evening, as Luna and Iris gazed up at the stars, something magical happened. A shooting star streaked across the sky. Luna, ever the dreamer, made a wish.

"I wish we could visit the stars," Luna said, her eyes shining with wonder.

Iris, with her wise and knowing gaze, nodded. "Then let us embark on a starlight voyage."

With that, Luna and Iris felt like they were being lifted off the ground and carried by the shimmering stardust. They soared high into the night sky, leaving the town of Serendipity Springs far below. Around them, constellations came to life, each one taking on a unique form and personality.

First, they met Orion, the great hunter of the heavens. He was strong and brave, with a belt made of three bright stars. Orion shared tales of his adventures among the stars and taught Luna and Iris that courage could guide one through even the darkest of nights.

Next, they encountered Cassiopeia, the queen of the constellations. She sat on her celestial throne with grace and dignity. Cassiopeia spoke of the importance of balance and harmony in all things, reminding Luna and Iris that finding balance in life was a journey worth pursuing.

As Luna and Iris continued their starlight voyage, they met countless other constellations, each with their own stories and wisdom to share. The Little Dipper, with its gentle glow, taught them about the beauty of simplicity. And Draco the dragon, with his winding form across the sky, revealed the power of transformation.

Finally, they arrived at the North Star, Polaris, which shone brightly and steadily above all others. Polaris guided the travelers on their journeys, as the dreams guided Luna and Iris. Polaris encouraged them to follow their dreams with determination and trust in their hearts.

With these newfound insights, Luna and Iris thanked the constellations for their wisdom and bid them farewell. They returned to Serendipity Springs, their hearts full of wonder and their minds illuminated by the knowledge of the stars.

From that night on, Luna and Iris knew that dreams were not just fleeting wishes but guiding lights, like the stars themselves. They understood that each constellation in the sky tells a story, just as every person's life is a story waiting to be lived.

And so, Luna and Iris continued their adventures, knowing that the starlight would always be there to guide them on their journey.

35

The Lost Melody

Luna and Iris come across a forgotten melody that has the power to heal hearts. They learn about the significance of music in connecting people and bringing joy to life.

Once upon a time, in a world not unlike our own, Luna and Iris found themselves wandering through a quiet forest. The trees seemed to whisper secrets to one another, their leaves rustling softly in the breeze. Birds sang songs that sounded like laughter, and the air was filled with an aura of tranquility.

As they strolled deeper into the woods, Luna noticed something unusual. Among the harmonious sounds of nature, a hauntingly beautiful melody rumbled in the air. It was a melody unlike any they had heard before, both sad and sweet, like a distant memory of joy.

Intrigued, Luna and Iris followed the melody, their curiosity piqued. They ventured deeper into the forest until they stumbled upon a clearing where a small, forgotten music box lay. The music box was old and worn, its wooden exterior adorned with intricate carvings of animals, stars, and crescent moons.

Luna, with her keen feline senses, nudged the music box gently. It creaked open, and the haunting melody swelled, filling the clearing with its melancholic beauty. Luna and Iris sat down beside the music box; their hearts captured by the enchanting tune.

The melody told a story of lost love, of a heart that had been wounded but still held hope. It spoke of the healing power of music, how it could mend even the deepest of scars. Luna and Iris closed their eyes, letting the melody wash over them. At that moment, they felt a profound sense of connection.

As the last note of the melody faded away, Luna and Iris knew they had to share this precious gift with others. They carefully closed the music box, tucking it under Luna's arm, and began their journey back through the forest.

They played the music box's melody as they walked, letting it weave its magic through the forest. Birds began to sing along, and the trees rustled in time with the tune. Soon, other animals joined in, and the once-quiet forest became a symphony of sound and life.

Luna and Iris continued to share the lost melody as they traveled through villages and towns. Everywhere they went, hearts were touched, and spirits were lifted. The power of music to heal and connect people became evident, and Luna and Iris felt a deep sense of fulfillment.

Their journey with the lost melody taught them that even the most forgotten and neglected things could hold immense beauty and power. It also reminded them of the importance of sharing such treasures with the world, for in doing so, they could bring joy, healing, and connection to others.

Luna and Iris carried the music box with them as they continued their adventures, and shared its lost melody wherever they went. They knew the world was full of forgotten treasures waiting to be discovered, and they were eager to uncover them all.

36

The Island of Reflection

Luna and Iris encounter an island with mystical mirrors that reveal inner truths. They discover the importance of self-reflection and self-acceptance on their adventure.

Once upon a time, in a world where wonders knew no bounds, Luna and Iris embarked on a new adventure. It was a clear, sunny morning when they set sail, their little boat gliding through the azure waters. As they sailed further, a peculiar island came into view. This island was covered with mirrors, mirrors of all shapes and sizes, glistening like diamonds in the sun.

"Look at that, Luna," Iris said, her eyes wide with wonder. "It's as if the whole island is covered in mirrors!"

Luna, always open to the mysteries of their world, couldn't help but smile. "It's beautiful, Iris. Let's go take a closer look."

They sailed their boat to the island's shores, and as they disembarked, they soon realized that these were not ordinary mirrors. When Luna gazed into one, it didn't reflect her physical appearance. Instead, it revealed something much deeper—their innermost thoughts and feelings.

As Luna peered into one mirror, she saw a moment from her past when she had felt intense fear. But as she continued to watch, she saw how she had summoned courage from within, facing her fear head-on. Her heart swelled with pride as she realized that even during her most vulnerable moments, she had the strength to overcome.

Iris, too, was captivated by the mirrors. She looked into one and saw a time when she had doubted herself, questioning whether she was capable of great things. But as she continued to watch, she saw herself rising above those doubts, discovering her strength and determination.

The mirrors on the Island of Reflection were like magical windows into their souls, offering glimpses of their innermost selves. They didn't just show moments of vulnerability; they also revealed moments of triumph, love, and joy.

As Luna and Iris explored further, they began to understand that these mirrors were meant to teach them something valuable about self-reflection and self-acceptance. They were like guides on a journey into their hearts and minds.

The day passed swiftly as they looked into mirror after mirror, learning from their reflections. Luna realized that embracing her past, including moments of fear and doubt, was a part of what made her who she is today. It was all connected, like pieces of a grand puzzle coming together.

Iris discovered that it was okay to have vulnerabilities; they were a part of her uniqueness, making her stronger, not weaker. As she watched her reflection, she felt an overwhelming sense of self-compassion and self-acceptance.

As the setting sun painted the sky orange and pink, Luna and Iris sat on the sandy shore, mesmerized by the twinkling stars above. Looking up at the night sky, they realized that just like the mirrors, the night sky held a reflection of their essence. Each star represented a part of themselves—bright and unique.

With their newfound wisdom, Luna and Iris understood that self-reflection was not about dwelling on past mistakes or insecurities. It was about embracing every part of themselves—the light and the shadow, the triumphs and the struggles. Just like the mirrors, they were a beautiful mosaic of experiences and emotions.

Before they left the island, Luna and Iris left a note of gratitude to the mystical mirrors. As they sailed away, they felt lighter, freer, and more at peace with themselves. The Island of Reflection had gifted them a precious lesson in self-acceptance, one they knew they would carry with them on their continuing adventures.

37

The Timeless Clock Tower

Luna and Iris discover a clock tower that controls time itself. They learn about the preciousness of time and how to make the most of each moment.

Once upon a time, in a land where the wind whispered secrets through the ancient trees and the sun painted the sky with golden hues, Luna and Iris found themselves on the path to the Timeless Clock Tower. Their journey was guided by the gentle notes of a songbird that seemed to echo with a rhythm only they could hear.

As they approached the clock tower, its tall, glistening spire seemed to touch the very heavens. Its face was decorated with intricate hands that moved in perfect harmony, like a delicate ballet of time itself. Luna and Iris couldn't help but feel a sense of wonder as they drew nearer.

Upon entering the clock tower, Luna and Iris found themselves in a room filled with the soft ticking of countless clocks. Each one was different, telling a unique story of a moment in time. Some ticked slowly, savoring every second, while others raced ahead as if eager to embrace the future.

In the center of the room stood the grandest clock of them all. Its face was adorned with celestial patterns, and its hands moved with a grace that transcended mortal understanding. As Luna and Iris approached, they realized that this clock controlled time itself.

The guardian of the Timeless Clock Tower, an ancient and wise owl named Orion, greeted them. "Welcome, young travelers," he hooted, his eyes filled with the wisdom of ages. "I am Orion, the keeper of this clock, and I am here to teach you the preciousness of time."

With a gentle touch of his wing, Luna and Iris were transported into a world where they could witness moments from their own lives. They saw laughter shared with friends, quiet moments of reflection, and the beauty of a sunrise painting the sky. They also saw moments they wished they had cherished more, like a forgotten hug from a loved one or a breathtaking sunset left unwatched.

The owl spoke again, "Time is a gift, and each moment is a precious jewel. It is not the quantity of time you have but how you spend it that matters. Embrace each moment, for it will never come again."

Luna and Iris nodded, their hearts filled with understanding. They realized that life was not about racing against the clock but about savoring every tick. As they left the Timeless Clock Tower, the songbird's melody guided them back on their journey.

With newfound wisdom, Luna and Iris continued their adventures, cherishing every moment as they embraced the world around them. They knew that time was a gift, and they would make the most of every moment, no matter how fleeting.

The clock tower still stood tall, its hands moving gracefully, reminding all who encountered it of the beauty and fragility of time. Luna and Iris's hearts were forever touched by the lesson they had learned, and they carried it with them as they explored the wonders of their world.

And so, the story of Luna and Iris's encounter with the Timeless Clock Tower became a tale shared throughout the land, a reminder to treasure the moments that make life truly magical.

38
The Ocean of Dreams

Luna and Iris set sail on an ocean that carries dreams to distant shores. They learn about the interconnectedness of dreams and how they can shape the world.

Once upon a time, in the land of wonders, Luna and Iris found themselves standing at the edge of an immense ocean. It shimmered with the colors of dreams—vibrant purples, soothing blues, and gleaming golds. It was the Ocean of Dreams.

Luna and Iris, during their previous adventures, had heard whispers about this mystical place. And now, their curiosity led them to this extraordinary realm. As they gazed at the ocean's surface, they noticed that it was not water that flowed there but rather a soft and glowing ethereal mist.

A huge sailboat awaited them, decorated with intricate patterns that seemed to shift and change with every passing moment. Luna and Iris stepped aboard, and with a gentle gust of wind, the boat set sail upon the luminous sea.

As they glided across the Ocean of Dreams, Luna and Iris marveled at the dreamscape around them. Islands of varying sizes floated on the surface, each hosting unique scenes. On one island, children were laughing and playing, surrounded by candy-colored clouds. On another, artists painted the sky with brilliant strokes of color. Everywhere they looked, dreams came to life.

"Isn't it magical, Luna?" Iris asked, her eyes gleaming with wonder.

Luna nodded, her heart brimming with joy. "It was as if we had entered a world where the dreams of all living beings are intertwined."

The boat carried them to an island that shimmered like a diamond. On it stood a grand library, its shelves stretching far into the sky. Luna and Iris disembarked and ventured inside.

Within the library, books floated in mid-air, and as Luna and Iris approached, the books opened and began to tell their stories. These were not just any stories, though: they were dreams. Each book held the essence of someone's deepest aspirations, their most cherished desires, and their boundless imagination.

Luna and Iris picked up one of the dream books, and as they read, they felt themselves becoming part of the dreamer's story. They soared through the sky, danced with fireflies, and ventured into uncharted lands.

They realized that dreams held immense power, no matter how big or small they were. Dreams could unite people, inspire change, and shape the world. Luna and Iris felt a profound connection with the dreamers whose stories they had shared.

As they left the library, Luna and Iris knew that they had learned a valuable lesson. Dreams were not solitary, disconnected entities; they were threads woven into the fabric of existence, forming a tapestry of shared hopes and aspirations. When people believed in their dreams and worked together, the world could transform into a place of incredible beauty and wonder.

With newfound wisdom, Luna and Iris sailed back across the Ocean of Dreams. They knew that the tales they carried with them would inspire others to dream big and embrace their own innermost desires. And it motivates others to join forces in creating a world filled with love, compassion, and endless possibilities.

And so, Luna and Iris continued their journey, their hearts filled with gratitude for the enchanting Ocean of Dreams and the dreams they had encountered along the way.

39
The Crystal Caves

Luna and Iris explore caves filled with glowing crystals that hold memories of ancient civilizations. They uncover the wisdom of the past and its relevance in the present.

Once upon a time, Luna and Iris found themselves on the edge of a dense forest, their curiosity pulling them deeper into the unknown. As they ventured further, the trees seemed to whisper secrets, and the air was thick with an ancient mystique. Their steps were guided by an invisible hand, leading them to a place untouched by time itself, the Crystal Caves.

The entrance to the caves was a majestic sight. Glistening crystals of every color imaginable adorned the cave walls, casting a soft, ethereal glow that illuminated their path. It was as if they had entered a realm where dreams and memories merged into one.

Luna and Iris approached the nearest crystal, its radiance pulling them closer. As they touched it, a rush of memories coursed through their minds. They saw ancient civilizations, their hopes, dreams, and challenges. They witnessed acts of love and moments of courage, all encapsulated within the crystal's vibrant hues.

The crystals didn't just hold memories; they held the collective wisdom of those who had come before. Luna and Iris realized that they were in the presence of something profound: a living library of knowledge and experience.

Together, they explored the cave, each crystal revealing a different story. They learned about the power of unity from a crystal that shimmered with the memory of a diverse society living in harmony. Another crystal showed them the importance of courage as they watched a lone individual stand up against injustice.

As Luna and Iris journeyed deeper into the caves, they began to understand the interconnectedness of all things. Every memory, every story, was a thread in the tapestry of existence. They learned that the wisdom of the past was not confined to history books but lived on in the hearts and minds of those who remembered.

In one chamber, they discovered a crystal that pulsed with the memory of a wise elder teaching a child about the cycles of nature. It reminded them of the importance of respecting the earth and the delicate balance of life. They knew that this wisdom was as relevant in their time as it had been in the past.

Luna and Iris absorbed more knowledge and insight with each crystal they encountered. They realized that the past held keys to understanding the present and shaping the future. The Crystal Caves became a treasure trove of wisdom, a timeless sanctuary where the echoes of generations whispered their truths.

As they left the caves, their hearts felt lighter, filled with the wisdom and stories of the ancients. They knew that the crystals had gifted them a precious legacy—an understanding that would guide them on their journey of inner discovery and transformation.

And so, Luna and Iris emerged from the Crystal Caves, their spirits lifted by the profound lessons they had learned. They knew that they carried with them the wisdom of the ages, a beacon of light to illuminate the path ahead.

40

The Carnival of Emotions

Luna and Iris attend a magical carnival where emotions take center stage. They learn about the importance of embracing all emotions and how they contribute to a colorful life.

Once upon a time, in the enchanting world of Luna and Iris, a vibrant and bustling carnival appeared in the heart of the mystical forest. Luna and Iris were drawn to the carnival's kaleidoscope of colors, its melodic music, and the enticing aroma of sweet treats in the air.

As they stepped into the carnival, Luna and Iris noticed that something extraordinary was happening. Emotions had come to life and taken center stage! Joy, sadness, anger, fear, and love were all personified, each with its booth and activities.

The first booth they encountered was the Joyful Jamboree. A lively, giggly character named Joy was leading a dance party. Luna and Iris joined in, feeling their spirits lift as they danced with abandon. They realized that joy was not just about being happy but also about celebrating life's simple pleasures.

Next, they ventured into the Chamber of Sadness. Luna and Iris met a gentle, teary-eyed character named Sadie. She explained that sadness wasn't something to be avoided but a natural part of life. Sadie showed them that allowing oneself to feel sadness could lead to healing and growth.

They moved on to the Fire of Anger booth, where a fiery character named Blaze was passionately discussing important issues. Luna and Iris learned that anger, when channeled constructively, could be a powerful force for change. It was a reminder that standing up for what one believed in was essential.

Their journey then took them to the House of Fear, where a cautious character named Felix shared tales of courage. Luna and Iris discovered that acknowledging their fears could lead to bravery and personal growth. They realized fear was a vital part of the journey toward self-discovery.

Lastly, they arrived at the Garden of Love, where a character named Amora radiated warmth and compassion. Luna and Iris understood that love was the foundation of all emotions, the thread that connected everything in life. Love mends broken hearts, it could heal wounds, and create a world filled with understanding and empathy.

As Luna and Iris continued their adventure through the Carnival of Emotions, they discovered that all emotions played a significant role in their life experiences. Embracing each emotion allowed them to lead a more colorful, fulfilling life.

With newfound wisdom, Luna and Iris left the carnival, their hearts full of gratitude for the magical experience. They realized that emotions, like the colors of a rainbow, made life beautiful and meaningful.

And so, they continued their journey, knowing that every emotion they encountered was a gift, a piece of the intricate puzzle of their inner world.

41

The Enchanted Forest of Dreams

Luna and Iris venture into a mystical forest where dreams take on physical forms. They learn about the power of dreaming and how dreams can guide one's destiny.

Once upon a time, in a world not so different from our own, there existed a place known as the Enchanted Forest of Dreams. It was no ordinary forest. It was a place where dreams took on physical forms, where the line between the waking world and the world of dreams were blurred and intertwined.

Luna and Iris had heard whispers of this mystical forest during their travels. They were drawn to it like moths to a flame, curious to explore its wonders and secrets. So, one bright morning, they set off through dense woods, following a path illuminated by dappled sunlight.

As they ventured deeper into the forest, they noticed something extraordinary. Dreams hung in the air like gossamer threads, their colors and shapes as vivid as a painter's palette. Luna reached out and touched one, and it transformed into a radiant butterfly, fluttering around them before disappearing into the foliage.

"This place is unlike anything we've ever seen," Luna marveled.

Iris nodded in agreement. "It's as if the dreams themselves are alive here."

They continued their journey, and with every step, the forest seemed to come alive. Trees whispered ancient stories, and flowers sang songs of forgotten love. A river, crystal clear and filled with shimmering fish, flowed through the heart of the forest. It was said that if you dipped your hand into its waters, you could glimpse your dreams.

Luna and Iris decided to try. They knelt by the riverbank, cupped their hands, and dipped them into the cool, inviting water. As they gazed into the ripples, their reflections changed. Luna saw herself soaring through the skies on the back of a dragon. Iris saw herself dancing under a starry sky with fireflies as her partner.

"Look, Iris, it's our dreams," Luna whispered in awe.

The forest pulled them in with its dreamy embrace, guiding them further. They came upon a grove where dreams had taken root. Here, they found a tree with leaves that glowed like embers. Each leaf held a single dream, a cherished desire, a long-forgotten memory, or a glimpse into the future.

Luna plucked a leaf from the tree. It transformed into a radiant star. She made a wish upon it, and the star soared into the sky, leaving a trail of golden light behind.

"What did you wish for?" Iris asked.

Luna smiled. "I wished for the happiness of all living beings."

With that, they continued their journey, knowing that their encounter with the Enchanted Forest of Dreams had changed them forever. They had learned that dreams were not just fleeting thoughts. They were the guiding stars of one's destiny, the seeds of hope, and the essence of the human spirit.

As Luna and Iris emerged from the forest, they carried with them the magic of dreams. They knew that no matter how challenging their adventures became, they would always hold on to the dreams that lit their path through the Enchanted Forest.

And so, they continued their journey, ready to face whatever wonders and challenges lay ahead, their hearts filled with the knowledge that dreams can shape their destiny.

42

The Whimsical Playground of Imagination

Luna and Iris visit a magical playground where imagination knows no bounds. They learn about the importance of creativity and how it can unlock endless possibilities.

Once upon a time, in a world of dreams and possibilities, there lived a curious and adventurous cat named Luna. Luna was not an ordinary cat—she had a heart that yearned for exploration and a spirit that longed for new experiences.

Luna and Iris awoke one sunny morning to find themselves standing in front of the most peculiar playground they had ever seen. It was a place where swings transformed into flying carpets, slides became enchanted tunnels, and the sand in the sandbox sparkled like stardust. But what made this playground truly unique was the boundless power of imagination that filled the air.

Children of all ages were scattered around the playground, each engaged in a different activity that fueled their creative minds. Some were building towering sandcastles, while others painted vivid masterpieces on the walls with giant brushes. Luna and Iris couldn't contain their excitement as they ventured deeper into this magical place.

The first thing Luna noticed was a group of children taking turns swinging on a swing set that soared high into the sky. But as they swung, they weren't merely going up and down. With each rise, they found themselves soaring over cities made of clouds, floating alongside colorful hot air balloons, and dancing with the birds. Luna and Iris hopped on a swing, and off they went on their very own skyward adventure, laughing all the way.

Next, they came across a fantastic slide. As Luna and Iris slid down, they entered the land of make-believe. They found themselves in a world filled with talking animals, where flowers sang songs and trees told stories. Luna and Iris joined in the fun, playing hide-and-seek with bunnies and having tea parties with wise old owls.

In another corner of the playground was the sandbox filled with shimmering sand. When Luna and Iris started building sandcastles, their creations didn't stay still. With a flicker of their imagination, their castles transformed into bustling kingdoms. They watched in awe as tiny sand people carried out their day-to-day activities in the miniature world they had built.

As they explored further, they stumbled upon an area where children were creating colorful chalk drawings on the ground. Luna and Iris joined in, and their chalk drawings came to life, forming portals to different worlds. They hopped from drawing to drawing, experiencing a variety of adventures, from underwater escapades with mermaids to journeys through enchanted forests with talking animals.

Throughout the day, Luna and Iris discovered that anything was possible in the Whimsical Playground of Imagination. They learned the true magic of creativity, how it could transport them to places they had only dreamed of and allow them to experience endless adventures.

Luna and Iris left the playground as the sun began to set. Their hearts were full of wonder and inspiration. They realized that imagination was a treasure within them, ready to unlock countless possibilities whenever they wished.

With a newfound appreciation for creativity and the power of imagination, Luna and Iris knew they would carry the spirit of the Whimsical Playground of Imagination with them on all their future adventures.

43

The Garden of Resilience

Luna and Iris explore a garden where flowers symbolize different aspects of resilience. They learn about bouncing back from challenges and finding strength in adversity.

Once upon a time, in a world of dreams and possibilities, there lived a curious and adventurous cat named Luna. Luna was not an ordinary cat—she had a heart that yearned for exploration and a spirit that longed for new experiences.

In the heart of a magical forest, Luna and Iris stumbled upon the Garden of Resilience. It was a place where flowers held a unique story of resilience.

As Luna and Iris entered the garden, they were greeted by the sight of the most magnificent blooms they had ever seen; each one represented a different aspect of resilience.

The first flower they encountered was a radiant sunflower. It stood tall, basking in the sunlight. Its story was one of unwavering determination. Despite the challenges of rocky soil and harsh weather, it stretched towards the sun, always seeking the light. Luna and Iris learned that resilience was about staying focused on your goals, no matter the obstacles.

Next, they found a delicate rose with thorns. This flower symbolized strength in vulnerability. The rose had been through storms and rough winds, but its petals remained soft and beautiful. It taught Luna and Iris that resilience wasn't about being tough all the time; it was also about embracing your vulnerabilities.

Further into the garden, they discovered a daffodil. This flower had a cheerful, sunny disposition. It symbolized the power of positivity. The daffodil had faced adversity with a smile, teaching Luna and Iris that maintaining a positive outlook could help overcome even the darkest days.

As they continued their journey through the garden, Luna and Iris met a bamboo plant. Its story was one of flexibility. The bamboo could bend without breaking, even in the fiercest storms. It showed them that resilience meant being adaptable, bending with the winds of change, but never giving up.

Near a bubbling brook, they found a water lily. Its roots were planted firmly in the mud, but their pristine petals floated gracefully on the surface. The water lily symbolized finding peace amidst chaos. It taught Luna and Iris that true resilience could be found by staying calm and centered, no matter how turbulent life became.

Luna and Iris spent hours in the Garden of Resilience, learning from each unique flower they encountered. They realized that resilience wasn't just about toughness or never feeling pain. It was about embracing challenges, finding strength in vulnerability, staying positive, being adaptable, and finding peace amidst chaos.

When they left the garden, Luna and Iris took with them a deep understanding of resilience. They knew that life's challenges would come and go but with the lessons from the Garden of Resilience, they were better equipped to face them. And they were grateful for the wisdom this magical place shared with them.

44

The Sky's Art Gallery

Luna and Iris ascend to the sky and discover an art gallery where clouds create masterpieces. They learn about the beauty of impermanence and how every cloud painting is unique.

Once upon a time, Luna and Iris found themselves gazing at the sky, captivated by the ever-changing canvas of clouds above them. These clouds, however, weren't ordinary. They were artists in their own right, painting breathtaking masterpieces that danced across the heavens.

Luna and Iris decided to travel to the sky's art gallery, a place rumored to be hidden amidst the celestial realm. With hopeful hearts and a sense of wonder, they closed their eyes and imagined soaring high above the earth.

As their thoughts merged with the magic of the universe, Luna and Iris found themselves floating weightlessly among the clouds. It was an incredible sensation, feeling the cool breeze against their cheeks and the gentle touch of clouds beneath their feet.

Before them, the art gallery revealed itself, a shimmering expanse of boundless creativity. The clouds had taken on truly astonishing forms. Some resembled majestic mountains, their peaks reaching towards the sky. While others formed intricate patterns that resembled lacework. Each cloud painting seemed to tell a story of dreams and imagination.

Luna and Iris walked among the cloud creations, marveling at their ethereal beauty. They watched as wisps of cloud formed breathtaking landscapes that stretched as far as the eye could see. Mountains turned into valleys, rivers into oceans, and forests into deserts—all in the blink of an eye.

As they continued their journey, Luna and Iris noticed that the cloud paintings changed with every passing moment. They saw the sky painted fiery red and soft pink at sunset and deep blue and purple in the twilight hours. Each cloud masterpiece was a fleeting moment of artistry, a reminder that beauty could be found in impermanence.

The clouds seemed to sense Luna and Iris's presence and interacted with them. They swirled and danced around the two friends, creating patterns of astonishing complexity. Luna and Iris, too, began to express their creativity. They blew gentle winds through the clouds, causing ripples of color to cascade across the sky.

Hours passed like minutes in the celestial art gallery, and Luna and Iris knew they had to return to earth. They left the sky with hearts full of inspiration and a newfound appreciation for the fleeting beauty of each moment.

As they descended through the atmosphere, Luna and Iris carried with them the memory of the sky's art gallery. They realized that, much like the clouds, life itself was a canvas of constant change. Every moment was a masterpiece in its own right, meant to be cherished for what it was.

And so, Luna and Iris returned to their terrestrial world, grateful for the journey they had undertaken. As they looked up at the ever-changing sky, they knew that the art gallery of the heavens would always be there, a reminder of the beauty that could be found in the impermanence of life.

45

The Mirror of Reflection

Luna and Iris stumble upon a magical mirror that reflects their true selves. They learn about self acceptance and embracing one's authentic identity.

Once upon a time, in the heart of a lush forest, Luna and Iris found themselves on a winding path. The sunlight filtered through the emerald leaves, creating a mottled pattern on the ground. The gentle hum of nature's symphony enveloped them, and the air was filled with the sweet scent of wildflowers.

As Luna and Iris ventured deeper into the forest, they came across a clearing. At the center of this mystical glade stood a wondrous mirror, its frame adorned with intricate patterns that seemed to dance with ethereal light.

A soft, melodic hum radiated from it and a delicate mist enveloped its surface. Luna, her eyes aglow with curiosity, approached the mirror first. She saw a vision of her inner self, luminous and radiant. It was as if the mirror could peer into the depths of her soul. Her inner self reached out as if yearning to merge with her, to help her embrace the truth within.

Iris, intuitive and wise as always, sensed Luna's mixture of wonder and trepidation. She stepped closer, whispering gently, "Luna, don't be afraid. This mirror reveals not just our outward appearance, but also our inner essence, the core of who we are. It's a gift, an opportunity to see the beauty and uniqueness within."

With Iris's reassuring words, Luna took a deep breath and gazed into the mirror once more. She saw all the stories that had shaped her—the trials and tribulations, the moments of joy and sorrow. Her inner self was a tapestry woven with threads of resilience, kindness, courage, and boundless curiosity.

Tears welled up in Luna's eyes. She realized that all the facets of her being, even the ones she had once considered flaws, were part of her unique tapestry. Luna smiled at her reflection, feeling the warmth of self-love envelop her like a soft, comforting embrace.

Iris, witnessing Luna's transformation, couldn't help but smile too. She knew that this experience would be a turning point in Luna's journey. It was a lesson in embracing one's authentic self and celebrating the beautiful mosaic of one's existence.

With newfound clarity and self-acceptance, Luna turned to Iris, "Iris, thank you for being my guide on this incredible journey. Through this mirror, I've learned that embracing my true self is the key to unlocking my full potential."

Iris replied, "Luna, we are all mirrors, reflecting the beauty and uniqueness within each other. Remember this lesson as we continue our adventures together."

As Luna and Iris left the magical mirror behind, they carried with them the wisdom of self-acceptance and the knowledge that their authentic selves were their greatest treasures. The forest seemed to whisper its approval as if celebrating their newfound understanding, and a soft breeze rustled the leaves.

With every step they took, Luna and Iris felt a profound connection not only to each other but to the world around them. They knew that their journey was far from over, but armed with self-love and the lessons of the mystical mirror, they were ready to face whatever adventures lay ahead.

46

The Garden of Echoing Whispers

Luna and Iris stumble upon a hidden garden where every whisper of kindness sprouts into vibrant, talking flowers. They learn about the magical resonance of kindness and how even the tiniest acts can change destinies.

Once upon a time, in a world of dreams and possibilities, there lived a curious and adventurous cat named Luna. Luna was not an ordinary cat—she had a heart that yearned for exploration and a spirit that longed for new experiences.

One day, Luna and Iris wandered through the forest; the sun dappling through the leaves and casting a gentle glow on their path. Birds serenaded them with cheerful melodies, and a soft breeze carried with it the scent of wildflowers. As they walked deeper into the woods, the air seemed to shimmer with an otherworldly quality.

Soon, they came upon a small, unassuming garden hidden amidst the trees. Luna and Iris exchanged curious glances before stepping inside. What they saw took their breath away.

The garden was full of vibrant flowers of every shape and color lined the path, their petals whispering in the breeze. Luna and Iris approached a particularly striking crimson bloom.

"Hello," Iris said, her voice barely above a whisper.

The flower responded, its petals quivering with life. "Hello, dear travelers," it replied in a delicate, musical voice.

Luna couldn't believe her eyes. "It can talk!"

The flower nodded. "Indeed, we all can. In this garden, every act of kindness, every whispered word of love, every gentle touch gives life to a new flower. And we, the flowers of echoing whispers, are the living testament to the kindness in the hearts of those who visit."

Luna and Iris were enchanted. They spent hours in the garden, listening to the tales of the flowers. Each bloom had its own unique story to tell, each one born from an act of kindness. They heard stories of strangers helping strangers, friends lifting each other up, and countless small gestures that had rippled into great waves of good.

One particularly radiant sunflower spoke of a little girl who had planted it in the garden after sharing her toys with a lonely child. Another, a delicate bluebell, told the story of a musician who had played a heartwarming tune for a grieving friend, the notes taking flight and blooming into flowers.

As they wandered deeper into the garden, Luna and Iris realized that their presence had brought forth new blossoms. Flowers sprang up wherever they went, echoing their laughter and kindness.

"This place is magical," Luna said with wonder. "It reminds us of the importance of kindness, of the incredible impact even the smallest acts can have."

Iris nodded, her heart brimming with joy. "And the echoes of our good deeds can resonate far beyond what we can see."

The flowers of the garden nodded in agreement. "Kindness is like a seed. Plant it in the world, and watch as it blooms into a garden of echoing whispers, a testament to the beauty of the heart."

With their hearts full of gratitude, Luna and Iris bid farewell to the garden, knowing that they would carry its lessons with them on their journey. As they left, the flowers whispered blessings of kindness, their voices echoing in the breeze.

And so, Luna and Iris left, knowing that every act of kindness they sowed in the world would echo back to them, creating a tapestry of love and beauty wherever they roamed.

47

The Chromatic Kaleidoscope

Luna and Iris wander into a kaleidoscopic forest where colors come alive to narrate stories through living art. They uncover the significance of embracing a world painted in diverse hues, each with its own captivating story.

Once upon a time, in a world of dreams and possibilities, there lived a curious and adventurous cat named Luna, and her friend Iris, the butterfly.

One day, Luna and Iris found themselves surrounded by a kaleidoscope of colors. Trees, flowers, and even the air seemed to shimmer with an iridescent glow. The world around them was alive with vibrant hues, each one telling a unique and captivating story.

As they ventured deeper into the kaleidoscopic forest, Luna and Iris encountered a tree with leaves that shifted from emerald green to deep indigo. The leaves rustled in the breeze, and Luna reached out to touch one. To their amazement, the leaf transformed into a delicate butterfly, its wings a mesmerizing blend of colors.

The butterfly fluttered in front of Luna and Iris, its wings creating a mesmerizing dance of colors. It spoke in a soft and melodic voice, "I am the guardian of the Colorful Grove. Here, every color has a tale to tell. Will you listen?"

Luna and Iris nodded eagerly; their curiosity piqued. The butterfly began to weave a story with its wings, each movement revealing a different scene. The colors swirled and merged, forming images of far-off lands, mythical creatures, and everyday heroes.

As they listened to the butterfly's story, Luna and Iris were transported to the heart of each tale. They sailed on a sea of sapphire waves, soared through the skies on the wings of a majestic phoenix, and walked alongside brave adventurers who faced incredible challenges.

The butterfly's tale continued, and Luna and Iris saw how the colors represented emotions, experiences, and the diversity of life itself. Every shade, from the warmest red to the coolest blue played a crucial role in the world's grand tapestry.

"We are all part of the same kaleidoscope," the butterfly said, "and our stories are intertwined. Just as the colors blend and merge, so do our lives."

Luna and Iris felt a deep connection to the world around them. They realized that embracing diversity and appreciating the unique stories of every individual was essential to creating a harmonious world.

With gratitude in their hearts, Luna and Iris bid farewell to the Colorful Grove and the butterfly. As they continued their journey through the kaleidoscopic forest, they noticed how the colors seemed even more vibrant, and the world around them felt richer and more alive.

Luna and Iris encountered many more tales within the kaleidoscope forest. They met a jovial rainbow-colored squirrel who shared stories of unity and cooperation, a gentle bluebird who sang songs of peace and tranquility, and a wise old owl whose feathers changed colors as it recounted stories of wisdom and understanding.

With each story they heard, Luna and Iris's appreciation for the kaleidoscopic forest deepened. They marveled at how the colors could convey emotions and experiences that transcended language. In this magical place, differences were celebrated, and the beauty of diversity shone brightly.

As Luna and Iris left the kaleidoscopic forest behind, they carried with them a newfound understanding. They knew that the world was a vast tapestry of colors and each shade, no matter how subtle or bold, had a role to play in the grand design of life.

Back in their corner of the world, Luna and Iris shared the lessons they had learned with their friends and loved ones. They encouraged others to embrace the kaleidoscope of colors that make up their world and appreciate the unique stories that each individual brought to the tapestry of life.

Luna and Iris continued their adventures, knowing that the lessons of the kaleidoscopic forest would always guide their way. They understood that the beauty of life lay in its diversity and that every color, every story, and every individual contributed to the rich tapestry of existence.

48

The Elemental Harmony Quest

Luna and Iris set off on a quest to encounter elemental beings: the Flame Dancer, Aqua Siren, Terra Guardian, and Zephyr Muse. They explore the harmonious dance of these elements in nature, understanding how balance sustains the world.

One day, Luna and Iris found themselves at the edge of a dense, ancient forest. The trees whispered secrets of ages gone by, and the air was filled with an electrifying energy. As they ventured further into the woods, they began to feel the presence of something extraordinary.

Soon, they encountered a radiant figure dancing gracefully amid flames. It was the Flame Dancer, an elemental being of fire. She had fiery hair and her eyes sparkled like burning embers. Luna and Iris watched in awe as she twirled and leaped, her movements as mesmerizing as the dancing flames themselves.

The Flame Dancer beckoned them to join her. Luna hesitated at first, unsure of how to interact with such intense heat. But with Iris by her side, she found the courage to approach. As they danced together, Luna felt the warmth of the flames, not as a destructive force but as a symbol of passion and transformation.

After bidding farewell to the Flame Dancer, Luna and Iris journeyed further into the forest. They came upon a tranquil pond, where a beautiful Aqua Siren sang hauntingly sweet melodies. Her voice was like liquid silver, and the water danced in response to her song.

The Aqua Siren invited them to sit by the pond's edge and listen to her enchanting tunes. Luna and Iris closed their eyes, allowing the music to wash over them. It felt as though the melodies were cleansing their souls, filling them with a deep sense of tranquility and purity.

As they continued their quest, Luna and Iris encountered the Terra Guardian, a mighty elemental being of earth. She stood tall and resolute, her skin adorned with intricate patterns of vines and leaves. Luna and Iris marveled at her strength and stability.

The Terra Guardian welcomed them to explore her domain, where they discovered a lush, vibrant garden teeming with life. Luna knelt to touch the rich, fertile soil and felt a deep connection to the earth beneath her. The Terra Guardian explained that the balance of life depended on the nurturing embrace of the earth.

Their final encounter led them to the Zephyr Muse, a graceful being of air. She floated effortlessly through the sky, her laughter like the rustling of leaves in the wind. Luna and Iris joined her in a joyous dance through the clouds.

With each twirl, they felt the exhilarating freedom of the wind and understood how air could carry both whispers and roars. The Zephyr Muse reminded them that air was the breath of life, connecting all living beings.

As Luna and Iris concluded their journey and bid farewell to the Zephyr Muse, they realized the profound harmony that existed among these elemental beings. Fire, water, earth, and air—all different yet interconnected, each playing a vital role in maintaining balance in the natural world.

With newfound wisdom, they left the enchanted forest, knowing that the elements they had encountered were not just forces of nature but living entities with their own stories to tell. They had witnessed the elemental dance that sustained their world, leaving them with a deep appreciation for the delicate harmony of life.

49

The Empathy Chronicles

Luna and Iris enter a realm housing the Empathy Chronicles: books filled with dreams and experiences of individuals from a myriad of backgrounds. They embark on a journey of empathy and find that understanding diverse perspectives enriches their own lives.

Once upon a time, in a realm beyond our own, Luna and Iris found themselves in the realm of the Empathy Chronicles, a world where experiences and dreams were recorded in magical books.

The shelves reached higher than the tallest trees, and the books shimmered with an ethereal glow. These books that held within their pages the dreams, emotions, and stories of people from all walks of life.

Luna and Iris approached one of the books and as they opened it, they were instantly transported into the world of the dreamer. In that moment, they became that person, experiencing life from their perspective. It was a profound sensation as if they had stepped into someone else's shoes and were seeing the world through their eyes.

In one book, Luna found herself as a young artist living in a bustling city. She felt the struggles and triumphs of trying to make her passion into a career. In another, Iris inhabited the life of a skilled botanist, navigating the challenges of preserving rare and endangered plants.

Through these experiences, Luna and Iris began to understand the diverse perspectives that existed in the world. They realized that each person's journey is unique and filled with joys and sorrows, hopes and fears. It was a revelation that broadened their hearts and deepened their empathy.

As they continued to explore the library, Luna and Iris found themselves in stories from different cultures, periods, and circumstances. They walked in the shoes of farmers, explorers, musicians, and healers. They felt the love of a parent, the thrill of a grand adventure, the ache of loss, and the resilience of the human spirit.

With each new story, Luna and Iris become more connected to the world around them. They understood that empathy was not just about feeling for others; it was about feeling with them. It was about taking the time to truly listen and appreciate the beauty of each individual's journey.

When they finally left the Empathy Chronicles, Luna and Iris carried with them a profound sense of understanding and compassion. They knew that every person they met in their travels had a unique story to tell, and they were eager to hear those stories, to learn from them, and to share their own experiences in return.

And so, Luna and Iris continued their adventures with open hearts and a deeper sense of empathy. They knew that this newfound understanding would not only enrich their own lives but also the lives of those they met along the way.

50

The Guiding Beacon of Eternity

Luna and Iris stumble upon a timeless beacon that helps souls find their unique paths through eternity. They learn about the profound impact of guiding others on their journey and how it illuminates their own way.

Once upon a time, in a world of dreams and possibilities, there lived a curious and adventurous cat named Luna and her friend Iris. Luna was not an ordinary cat—she had a heart that yearned for exploration and a spirit that longed for new experiences.

One day, Luna and Iris had wandered deep into the heart of the mystical forest. The trees here stood tall and ancient, their branches reaching high into the sky as if they were trying to touch the heavens themselves. The air was filled with a serene stillness, and the whisper of leaves rustling in the wind seemed to lead the two friends deeper into the forest.

As they ventured further, they stumbled upon a clearing bathed in a warm, golden light. In the center of this clearing stood a magnificent, ancient lighthouse. It was unlike any lighthouse Luna and Iris had ever seen. Its tower was made of gleaming silver and decorated with intricate carvings that seemed to depict the entire history of the forest.

"What do you think this lighthouse is for?" Luna wondered aloud, her eyes wide with curiosity.

Iris, always the brave one, couldn't resist exploring. "Let's find out," she said, bounding ahead with Luna close behind.

When they reached the entrance to the lighthouse, they noticed a softly glowing inscription above the door: "The Guiding Beacon of Eternity."

Luna gently pushed the door open, and they entered a chamber bathed in a soft, ethereal light. The walls were adorned with countless paintings, each telling a unique story. Luna and Iris were drawn to a mural that depicted a soul, represented as a glowing sphere of light, embarking on a journey through time.

As they gazed at the mural a soft, melodic voice filled the room. "Welcome, travelers," it said. Luna and Iris looked around but saw no one.

"Who said that?" Luna asked, her eyes darting around.

The voice chuckled softly. "I am the keeper of this beacon, the guardian of souls on their eternal journey. I am here to guide you."

Luna and Iris exchanged glances; their curiosity piqued.

"You see," the voice continued, "this lighthouse is no ordinary one. It guides lost souls, helping them find their unique paths through eternity. Each painting on these walls tells the story of a soul's journey, and each soul that passes through here leaves its mark, adding to the ever-growing tapestry of existence."

Luna and Iris were captivated by the idea of a beacon that guided souls through eternity. It felt like a profound revelation, and they realized that it wasn't just about helping others find their way; it was also about illuminating their path.

"Can you show us more?" Luna asked, her voice filled with wonder.

The voice agreed and guided them through the lighthouse, sharing the stories of the souls whose journeys were depicted on the walls. Luna and Iris learned about the profound impact of guiding others on their path, and how it created ripples of love and kindness that echoed through eternity.

As they left the lighthouse, their hearts were filled with a newfound understanding of the importance of helping others find their way. They realized that by guiding others, they were also illuminating their own journey through life, leaving a trail of love and light behind them.

With this newfound wisdom, Luna and Iris continued their journey through the mystical forest, their steps guided by the light of the Guiding Beacon of Eternity.

51

The Symphony of Serenity

Luna and Iris visit a tranquil forest where each sound forms harmonious melodies. They learn about the importance of inner peace and how it resonates with the world around them.

One day, Luna and Iris had heard whispers of a serene forest, a place where every sound played a part in a harmonious symphony. Eager to discover the magic of this place, they set off early one morning, their steps light and their hearts full of curiosity.

A gentle breeze greeted them, rustling the leaves above them as they entered the forest. It sounded like a soothing lullaby, and Luna and Iris closed their eyes for a moment, taking in the peaceful melody.

The forest was alive with sounds. Birds sang sweetly from the treetops while a nearby stream gurgled softly as it meandered through the mossy rocks. The insects provided a rhythmic chorus with their buzzing and chirping.

Luna and Iris walked deeper into the forest, their footsteps adding a gentle percussion to the symphony. They noticed that every note, no matter how small or seemingly insignificant, had its place and purpose in this beautiful composition.

They approached a clearing where the sunlight filtered through the leaves and made a mottled pattern on the forest floor. In the center of the clearing stood a majestic oak tree. Its branches swayed in time with the forest's music. Under the tree sat an old man with a long, white beard, his eyes closed in deep concentration.

In his lap, he held a small instrument that resembled a flute. The notes danced through the air, blending seamlessly with the forest's natural sounds as he played. It was as if the forest itself was joining in his melody.

Luna and Iris watched in awe as the old man's music weaved together with the sounds of the forest. It was a symphony of serenity, a perfect harmony that resonated deep within their souls.

Curious, Luna and Iris approached the old man. He sensed their presence and opened his eyes, revealing a warm smile.

"Welcome, young travelers," he said, his voice as gentle as the wind. "I am Orin, and this forest is my home. Here, we create a symphony where every sound, no matter how subtle, contributes to the tranquility of this place."

Luna and Iris introduced themselves and intently listened as Orin shared the wisdom of the forest. He explained that in the Symphony of Serenity, each living being and each sound played a vital role. The birds' songs were like the violins, the babbling stream provided the rhythm, and the wind carried the melodies through the trees.

"But what is your role in this symphony?" Iris asked.

Orin smiled again and gestured to the small flute-like instrument in his hand. "I am the conductor," he replied. "I guide and harmonize the sounds of the forest, ensuring that they blend into a peaceful and harmonious composition."

As Orin continued to play his instrument, Luna and Iris understood the importance of inner peace and how it mirrored the symphony they witnessed. Like the forest, their hearts and minds needed balance and harmony to create a serene and beautiful life.

With gratitude in their hearts, Luna and Iris bid farewell to Orin and the Symphony of Serenity. As they walked back through the forest, they realized that inner peace was a tangible experience. They carried the memory of the forest's harmonious sounds with them, a reminder that serenity could be found within and around them in the symphony of life itself.

52

The Starlit Dreamscape

Luna and Iris embark on a celestial journey to explore dreams as constellations in the night sky. They discover the significance of following their own dreams and how they connect with the universe.

One clear and starry night, Luna and Iris found themselves in a dreamscape unlike any they had ever seen. They stood in an endless, twinkling expanse where dreams took on the form of constellations, painting the night sky.

The duo gazed in awe at the dreamscape, where the stars formed intricate patterns, each telling a unique story. Iris pointed to a constellation that resembled a majestic dragon, its wings outstretched in flight. "Look," she said with awe, "that's the Dream of Courage, where dreamers find the strength to face their fears."

Luna noticed a constellation in the shape of a blossoming flower, its petals unfurling gracefully. "And that," Luna added, "is the Dream of Growth, where one's aspirations and ambitions bloom like a beautiful flower."

They continued to explore this celestial dreamscape, each constellation revealing its profound meaning. They saw constellations of hearts intertwined, representing the Dream of Love, where the bonds between people were as enduring as the stars themselves. There were constellations of books and quills that created the Dream of Knowledge, where the thirst for wisdom led to endless discoveries.

As Luna and Iris ventured further into the dreamscape, they encountered a constellation that formed the shape of a winding path. It was the Dream of Destiny, guiding dreamers toward their true purpose. Luna and Iris looked at each other and smiled, understanding that they were on their own paths, guided by their dreams.

In the heart of the dreamscape, they discovered a constellation that resembled an outstretched hand offering help. It was the Dream of Unity, where dreamers learned how important it is to work together to achieve our dreams. Luna and Iris held hands, feeling the power of unity and shared dreams.

As they marveled at the starlit dreamscape, a constellation of a grand tree caught their attention. Its roots ran deep into the cosmos while its branches reached out to touch other constellations. It was the Dream of Connection. It reminds dreamers that they are part of a greater whole, connected to the universe itself.

Luna and Iris felt a profound sense of awe and gratitude for this dreamscape. They realized that every dream, no matter how small or grand, has its place in the night sky. Each dream was a beacon of hope and inspiration.

As they lay beneath the starlit canopy, Luna and Iris made a promise to follow their dreams, no matter where they led. They knew that their dreams were woven into the fabric of the universe, just like the constellations above.

With hearts full of hope and determination, Luna and Iris left the dreamscape, their dreams shining brightly within them and their spirits lifted by the starlit wonders of the universe.

53

The Enchanted Melody Meadow

Luna and Iris wander into a meadow where every flower emits a unique musical note. They learn about the power of creativity and how music can be a source of inspiration and unity.

Once upon a time, in a world of dreams and possibilities, there lived a curious and adventurous cat named Luna and her friend Iris.

One day, Luna and Iris found themselves on the edge of a meadow that stretched as far as the eye could see. The moment their feet touched the soft, emerald grass, a gentle breeze swept through the meadow, and a chorus of melodic notes filled the air. Each blade of grass, each flower, emitted a unique musical note.

Iris's eyes sparkled with wonder. "Luna, do you hear that? It's like the whole meadow is singing a song."

Luna nodded with a broad smile on her face. "I've never seen anything like this before, Iris. It's magical!"

They ventured further into the meadow, their steps creating harmonious tunes. Luna reached down to pluck a red rose, and as she held it, the petals produced soft, sweet notes that danced around her fingers.

Iris, not to be outdone, picked a daisy, which chimed in with cheerful, high-pitched tones. They laughed as they held their blossoms high, creating a charming duet of flowers and music.

As they explored deeper into the meadow, they encountered other flowers, each with its own musical signature. The tulips sang in a gentle, soothing lullaby while the sunflowers resonated with bright, cheerful melodies. Even the wild grasses contributed to the symphony with their soft, whispering harmonies.

Luna and Iris marveled at the unity and diversity of this meadow, where each flower, though unique, blended seamlessly into the enchanting melody. They realized that, just like in this meadow, the world was made richer by the diversity of its inhabitants. Their hearts swelled with gratitude for the beauty and harmony that surrounded them.

In the heart of the meadow, they found a majestic oak tree with leaves that rustled like a symphony of strings. Luna leaned against the tree, her eyes closed, and she listened to the soothing serenade. Iris sat beside her, the daisy she held now part of the grand composition.

Luna and Iris felt a deep sense of unity and inspiration when the sun slowly dipped below the horizon. They understood that just as the meadow's melodies blended to create a harmonious masterpiece, so did the diversity of the world's people and cultures creating a beautiful tapestry of humanity.

Hand in hand, Luna and Iris left the Enchanted Melody Meadow, their hearts filled with music, inspiration, and a newfound appreciation for the power of unity in diversity.

54

The Whispers of Wisdom

Luna and Iris discover an ancient tree that shares wisdom through its rustling leaves. They gain insights into the value of listening and learning from nature and the world around them.

Once upon a time, in a lush and ancient forest, Luna and Iris found themselves wandering deeper into the heart of nature. Birds sang melodic tunes, and the leaves of towering trees whispered secrets to the wind. The duo marveled at the beauty and serenity of the forest, feeling more connected to the natural world with each step.

As they strolled along a winding path, Luna noticed an old tree standing tall, its gnarled branches reaching toward the sky. Iris, always curious, encouraged Luna to approach the tree. The tree seemed to radiate wisdom, and its leaves rustled gently in the breeze.

Luna and Iris sat down at the base of the tree, their backs against its sturdy trunk. As they closed their eyes and listened to the gentle rustling of the leaves, they began to feel a deep sense of peace and connection with the forest. The tree seemed to sense their presence and started to share its wisdom.

"Listen, dear travelers," whispered the tree, "for the world around you has much to teach. The songs of the birds, the dance of the leaves, and the flow of the river all hold valuable lessons."

Luna and Iris listened intently with their hearts open to the wisdom of the tree. The tree continued, "In the quiet of nature, you will find answers to your questions, and in the stillness, you will discover the depths of your thoughts."

With these words, Luna and Iris felt a profound sense of peace and clarity wash over them. They realized that in the hustle and bustle of everyday life, they often overlooked the simple but essential lessons that nature offered.

As they sat there, embracing the wisdom of the ancient tree, they made a silent promise to spend more time in nature, to listen, learn, and connect with the world around them. They understood that the whisper of the wind and the rustle of the leaves contained profound guidance and inspiration.

With newfound insights, Luna and Iris thanked the wise tree and continued their journey through the forest. The lessons they had learned that day stayed with them, reminding them to always take the time to listen to the whispers of wisdom that nature had to offer.

And so, they walked hand in hand, their hearts filled with gratitude for the ancient tree and the valuable lessons it had shared. Their bond grew stronger as they ventured deeper into the forest, eager to discover more of nature's teachings.

55
The Cosmic Canvas

Luna and Iris venture into a realm where galaxies are painted on a vast cosmic canvas. They explore the infinite possibilities of the universe and the interconnectedness of all things.

Once upon a time, in a world of dreams and possibilities, there lived a curious and adventurous cat named Luna and her friend Iris.

One day, Luna and Iris stepped through a shimmering portal, finding themselves in a realm unlike any they had ever seen. Before them stretched a vast cosmic canvas adorned with galaxies of all shapes and sizes. It was a breathtaking sight, and Luna couldn't help but gasp.

"Look, Iris!" Luna whispered in awe. "It's like the entire universe is painted on this canvas."

Iris, her eyes filled with wonder, nodded in agreement. They approached the cosmic canvas. Luna reached out to touch one of the swirling galaxies. To her surprise, it emitted a soft, melodic hum.

"Listen," Luna said, her voice barely above a whisper.

They closed their eyes and let the cosmic melodies wash over them. It was as if the universe itself was speaking to them, telling stories of ancient civilizations, distant planets, and the birth of stars. Each galaxy had its unique tune, and together, they created a harmonious symphony that resonated with the very essence of the cosmos.

As they continued to explore, Luna and Iris noticed that some galaxies were connected by threads of shimmering light. It was a mesmerizing sight. Luna reached out to touch one of the threads, and it pulsed with energy. She could feel the interconnectedness of all things, the way every galaxy was linked to another in a cosmic dance.

"Luna," Iris said, her eyes filled with understanding, "this is the interconnectedness of the universe. Every galaxy, every star, every planet—they're all part of a grand design, a cosmic tapestry."

Luna nodded, her eyes shining with wisdom. She, too, felt the profound connection that flowed through the cosmic canvas. It was a reminder that they were never truly alone. And that they were part of something much larger than themselves.

As Luna and Iris continued their exploration, they encountered beings made of pure starlight. These celestial entities welcomed them with open arms, sharing their knowledge of the cosmos. They learned about the cycles of creation and destruction, the ebb and flow of energy, and the universe's infinite possibilities.

"We are all stardust," one of the celestial beings said, "born from the remnants of ancient stars. The same cosmic energy that birthed galaxies resides within each of you."

Luna and Iris felt a deep sense of gratitude for this cosmic revelation. They realized that they, too, were creators in their own right, capable of shaping their destinies and contributing to the ever-expanding tapestry of the universe.

As their journey through the realm of the cosmic canvas ended, Luna and Iris carried with them the melodies of the galaxies, the wisdom of the celestial beings, and a deep sense of interconnectedness. They knew that the universe was not just out there, but within them, guiding their every step.

With a final glance at the cosmic canvas, Luna and Iris stepped back through the shimmering portal, returning to their world. But they were forever changed, carrying the cosmic symphony in their hearts and the knowledge that they were, indeed, part of something extraordinary—a vast, interconnected cosmos that celebrated the beauty of diversity and unity.

56

The Garden of Gratitude

Luna and Iris stumble upon a garden where every plant represents a moment of gratitude. They learn about the transformative power of thankfulness and how it can bring positivity into their lives.

Once upon a time, Luna and Iris wandered through a vast and enchanted forest. The sun created a magical atmosphere by bathing everything in a warm, golden light. As they strolled deeper into the woods, they stumbled upon a hidden garden.

In this extraordinary garden, every plant represented a moment of gratitude. As Luna and Iris ventured further, and they noticed the plants were alive, moving gently in the breeze. These plants didn't just symbolize gratitude; they embodied it. The two friends marveled at the garden, feeling an overwhelming sense of serenity.

"Wow, Iris, this place is incredible," Luna whispered. "It's like every moment of gratitude has a home here, and each one is celebrated."

Iris, always keen to explore, nodded in agreement. "This is a profound reminder, Luna, of the power of gratitude. In our busy lives, we sometimes forget to appreciate the simple moments that fill our hearts with joy."

Luna reached out to touch one of the living plants, its petals soft and warm. "I understand, Iris. This gratitude is like a golden thread that weaves through the tapestry of our lives. Each moment we're thankful for adds another beautiful flower to the picture."

As Luna and Iris continued their walk, they noticed something truly remarkable: the more they expressed their gratitude, the more the garden seemed to come alive. Flowers began to bloom, and birds sang harmonious melodies overhead. Luna and Iris couldn't help but join in the symphony of gratitude. With every heartfelt word they spoke, new life sprouted from the earth.

Luna and Iris encountered a wise old tree as they continued through the garden. Its branches reached out like ancient, gnarled arms, and its leaves rustled with the stories of countless moments of gratitude. The tree seemed to glow with an inner light.

The tree whispered, "Welcome to the Garden of Gratitude, dear friends. In this sacred place, you have witnessed the transformative power of thankfulness. Gratitude is not just a feeling; it's a force that nourishes your soul and spreads its magic to the world around you."

Luna and Iris felt deeply moved by the wise tree's words. They sat beneath its branches and thought of all the things they were grateful for. Iris's heart was full as she reflected on the joy of the journey they were on, the wonders of nature, and the gift of friendship.

Luna expressed her gratitude for the opportunity to explore, learn, and grow every day; and for the beauty and harmony that surrounded them. The old tree's leaves rustled in contentment as the friends shared their feelings of thankfulness.

Before they left, Luna and Iris learned an important lesson: gratitude was a potent source of positivity and transformation. It had the power to turn the ordinary into the extraordinary.

With grateful hearts, they bid farewell to the Garden of Gratitude, their spirits lifted, and their souls enriched by the wisdom of the living garden.

57

The Chronicles of Courage

Luna and Iris find a library filled with stories of courageous individuals from different realms. They are inspired to face their fears and stand up for what they believe in.

Once upon a time, in a land where realms intertwined like threads of destiny, Luna and Iris embarked on a new quest. Their journey led them to a mysterious library hidden deep in an enchanted forest that housed chronicles of courage written about heroes from countless realms and worlds.

Luna and Iris entered the library, greeted by the scent of ancient parchment and the soft glow of candles floating mysteriously in the air. The room was vast, filled with towering bookshelves, each holding stories of courage and bravery. Luna marveled at the titles etched in gold and silver on the book spines, her tail flicking with curiosity, as Iris wove between the shelves.

As they approached the center of the library, they noticed a large tome resting on a pedestal, its cover adorned with illustrations of heroes in various forms—knights in shining armor, kind sorcerers, compassionate healers, and others.

Luna, unable to contain her curiosity, opened the book to a page that read, "The Tale of Ember the Fearless." The words leaped from the page, forming a lifelike image. The tale spoke of Ember, a small but fearless creature from the land of Fire and Ice.

Ember lived in a realm of eternal winter, where the inhabitants were locked in a never-ending battle to keep their fires burning. The world was harsh, and only the brave dared to venture into the icy wilderness. Ember, however, was unlike any other. Despite her diminutive size, her heart burned with unwavering courage.

The story recounted Ember's journey to find a fabled source of warmth, a quest that led her through treacherous landscapes and the frozen tundra. Her courage ignited the hearts of those around her, and they rallied together to brave the coldest of nights. They finally discovered the source of warmth was not in a hidden cave but within the bounds of their newfound unity.

As Luna and Iris read the story, they felt their spirits lifted. Ember's courage was infectious, and the narrative was a reminder of the importance of standing up for our beliefs and facing our fears.

Iris turned the page to reveal yet another hero's tale. This one told of a determined scientist from a realm of eternal darkness who sought to illuminate the world and bring hope to a place shrouded in perpetual night. The story painted a vivid picture of how courage could spark change in even the bleakest of circumstances.

Luna and Iris spent hours in the library, engrossed in the chronicles of courage, each tale leaving them more inspired than the last. As they left the library, they knew their hearts had been filled with a renewed sense of bravery, ready to face whatever challenges their adventurous journey had in store.

And so, with their spirits emboldened by the tales of courage they had discovered, Luna and Iris continued their quest, ready to stand up for what they believed in and face any fears that came their way.

58

The Time-Traveling Hourglass

Luna and Iris discover an hourglass that allows them to witness moments from the past and glimpse the future. They are understanding of the significance of living in the present.

Once upon a time, in the quaint little town of Celestia, Luna and Iris were out on one of their usual walks. They strolled through cobblestone streets, passed cozy cottages, and admired the vibrant gardens that filled the town with color.

As Luna and Iris ventured further, they came across an antique shop called "Elysian Treasures." It was a small, dusty shop with a rickety wooden sign swaying gently in the breeze. The shop had an aura of mystery about it as if it held secrets and stories from ages past.

Curiosity sparked in Luna's eyes, and Iris couldn't resist the lure of the unknown. They stepped inside, a little bell above the door announcing their entrance. The shop was dimly lit, and the air was filled with the smell of old books and memories.

Behind the counter stood an elderly woman, her silvery hair cascading like a waterfall, and her eyes sparkled with a wisdom that seemed to transcend time. Her name was Elara, and she was the owner of Elysian Treasures.

Luna and Iris were drawn to a peculiar object on the dusty shelf: an hourglass. The sand inside glimmered with an ethereal light, as if it held the essence of the past and the dreams of the future.

Intrigued, Luna and Iris asked Elara about the hourglass. She explained that it was the "Time-Traveling Hourglass," a magical artifact that allowed one to witness moments from the past and glimpse into the future. It was said to help people appreciate the significance of living in the present.

Elara handed the hourglass to Luna, who gazed at it in wonder. With Iris by her side, Luna gently turned the hourglass, and the sands began to flow.

The world around them shifted, and Luna and Iris found themselves in a bustling town square, surrounded by people dressed in vintage clothing, going about their daily lives. They were transported to the past, witnessing the history and stories of Celestia unfold before their eyes.

Luna marveled at the scenes from the past, from joyful celebrations to acts of kindness. As they observed the town's history, they gained a deep appreciation for the beauty of moments long gone.

When Luna and Iris turned the hourglass once more, the world around them transformed yet again. They now stood in a vibrant, futuristic world filled with marvels of technology and stunning architecture. The future of Celestia unfolded before them, inspiring awe and wonder.

Through this glimpse of the future, Luna and Iris realized the potential of what could be. They understood that the present was where they could shape the future and that the choices they made today would affect tomorrow's world.

With a newfound appreciation for the past and a sense of purpose for the future, Luna and Iris returned to the shop with the Time-Traveling Hourglass and handed it back to Elara. As they stepped out into the cobblestone streets, they felt a profound connection to the town, its history, and its potential future.

From that day forward, Luna and Iris cherished each moment they shared, knowing that their journey was enriched by the past and influenced the possibilities of the future. With the wisdom of the Time-Traveling Hourglass, they discovered the beauty of living in the present, appreciating every second of their extraordinary adventure.

59

The Aurora Symphony

Luna and Iris witness the Northern Lights transform into a breathtaking symphony of colors and sounds. They learn about the beauty of natural phenomena and how they can inspire creativity.

One day, Luna and Iris ventured north following rumors of a mesmerizing display in the night sky. As they journeyed through icy landscapes and snowy forests, the stars above them began to twinkle with excitement, casting a brilliant, otherworldly glow. The anticipation of witnessing the Northern Lights filled the air, and the two companions couldn't wait to experience this natural wonder for themselves.

One crisp evening, as the sun sank below the horizon, the Northern Lights began to weave their mystical dance across the skies. Radiant hues of emerald, amethyst, and sapphire intertwined in graceful patterns that seemed almost choreographed. Luna and Iris watched in awe as the colorful ribbons of light twisted and twirled, creating a celestial masterpiece. The play of colors across the dark canvas of the night sky was simply breathtaking.

But the enchantment didn't end with the visual display alone. As the auroras continued their mesmerizing performance, Luna and Iris became aware of something even more astonishing. The Northern Lights were producing music. Each ribbon of light emitted a melodic note, resonating through the silence of the winter night. As the colors changed, so did the harmonies, resulting in an ethereal symphony that echoed through the forest.

Curiosity and wonder led Luna and Iris further into the snowy wilderness, where the colors of the auroras seemed to dance more vividly, and the music became a celestial chorus. As they stood in a tranquil clearing, surrounded by tall snow-covered trees, they felt the vibrations of the music resonate deep within their souls. The symphony of the aurora was both haunting and enchanting, a melody that brought a sense of calm and belonging.

The auroras performed with grace that defied description, their light and sound mingling in a seamless dance of color and melody. Luna and Iris were entranced. They realized that the Northern Lights were a living work of art, a testament to the beauty and harmony of the natural world.

Nature, they understood, had a profound way of inspiring creativity and stirring the depths of one's imagination. Luna and Iris felt a connection to the cosmos, a bond with the universe itself. In this magical moment, they discovered that the beauty of natural phenomena held a unique power to inspire and evoke creativity in those who were willing to listen and observe.

Deciding to spend the night in this enchanted meadow, they lay on a bed of soft snow, gazing upward as the Northern Lights continued their mesmerizing performance. Their hearts were filled with gratitude for this remarkable experience, a gift from the universe itself.

As the night drew to a close, the auroras retreated into the starry expanse, leaving Luna and Iris with a newfound appreciation for the miracles of nature. They realized that the world was a vast canvas of inspiration, and every day was an opportunity to be moved by its beauty.

With hearts full of awe and wonder, they continued their journey, eager to explore the mysteries that awaited them in the vast world.

60

The Wisdom of Whales

Luna and Iris have an underwater adventure with a pod of wise whales. They discover the importance of communication and the wealth of knowledge that can be gained from listening to others.

Once upon a time, in a world of dreams and possibilities, there lived a curious and adventurous cat named Luna and her friend Iris.

One day, Luna and Iris set out on a new adventure guided by the enchanting melody of the waves. This time, the mysterious call of the ocean lured them into the depths, where they encountered a pod of whales.

The majestic creatures greeted the duo with great wisdom in their eyes and kindness in their hearts. Luna and Iris listened intently, eager to learn the secrets of the underwater world.

The whales told stories of their long journeys across the vast oceans, their harmonious communication, and the importance of working together. Luna and Iris discovered that these gentle giants held the collective knowledge of their ancestors and shared this wisdom with the world.

As the day turned into night, the whales invited Luna and Iris to join them in a display of bioluminescence. With each flick of their tails, the sea came alive with a mesmerizing symphony of colors. The beauty of this spectacle took Luna and Iris's breath away.

Amidst the radiant lights, the whales communicated through a language of sounds and songs, forming a harmonious orchestra of the deep. Luna and Iris were struck by the power of effective communication and understanding.

The moon cast a silvery light on the ocean, and the whales continued their tales. They spoke of their role in maintaining the balance of the seas, the deep connections they shared with other sea creatures, and the urgency of preserving their delicate habitats.

Luna and Iris couldn't help but feel a profound connection to these wise beings. They learned that by listening to others, no matter how different they might seem, they could gain insight into the complexities of life. The gentle giants taught Luna and Iris to appreciate the beauty of unity and the value of preserving the oceans for generations to come.

With gratitude in their hearts, Luna and Iris bid farewell to their newfound friends, carrying the wisdom of the whales with them. As they resurfaced from their underwater adventure, they realized that communication, understanding, and unity could create harmony in their own lives.

61

The Celestial Serenade

Luna and Iris embark on a celestial journey to discover the music of the cosmos and its connection to life on earth.

Once upon a time, in a quiet corner of the garden, Luna and Iris found themselves gazing at the night sky. The stars sparkled like a myriad of precious gems, and the moon bathed the world in a silvery glow. Luna, the blue cat, and Iris, the butterfly, were friends bound by their unending curiosity and an unquenchable thirst for adventure.

"Look, Iris," Luna purred excitedly, her eyes fixed on the twinkling constellations above. "I've heard tales that the stars have their melodies. What do you think they sound like?"

Iris fluttered closer, her iridescent wings shimmering in the moonlight. "I've often wondered the same thing, Luna. Just imagine, if we could somehow unlock the celestial secrets of the cosmos, we might hear the most beautiful music in the universe."

With their hearts set on this new adventure, Luna and Iris began to explore the garden for clues on how to tune in to the celestial symphony. The journey led them to a hidden grove where ancient trees stood like sentinels. It was a magical place, bathed in silver moonlight.

In the heart of the grove, they found a mysterious wooden harp that seemed to have grown from the trees themselves. Luna gently tapped the strings, producing a delicate sound that resonated with the whispers of the wind. Iris watched in awe as Luna's playful tune attracted the attention of the fireflies, who danced around them in perfect harmony.

"Perhaps this harp can help us communicate with the stars," Iris whispered, her wings quivering with excitement. She landed delicately on one of the harp's strings, and the sound it produced was unlike anything they had ever heard.

The enchanting melody seemed to ripple through the night sky, and suddenly, the stars above began to twinkle and emit soft, ethereal notes. It was as if the universe itself had decided to join in their serenade.

The pair continued to pluck and stroke the harp's strings, learning to play in harmony with the stars. Each note they produced was met with a celestial response, and Luna and Iris soon found themselves surrounded by a celestial orchestra. Shooting stars streaked across the night sky, creating radiant streaks of light that danced in time with their music.

As the night deepened, the celestial serenade became more profound. Luna and Iris could feel the music resonating deep within their souls. It was as if the universe was sharing its secrets through this celestial language. In those moments, they deeply understood the interconnectedness of all life on earth and in the cosmos.

"We've unlocked the celestial serenade, Luna!" Iris exclaimed, her eyes reflecting the wonder of the universe. "This music is a reminder that we are a part of something greater, something infinite and beautiful."

Luna nodded in agreement, a contented purr escaping her. "Indeed, Iris. We've discovered that the music of the cosmos is not only beautiful but a reminder of the harmony that exists within the universe."

As the night waned, Luna and Iris continued their serenade. They knew that their celestial discovery was a gift they would carry with them forever. It reminded them of the profound connection between the earth and the cosmos.

With this newfound knowledge and sense of wonder, they returned to the garden, their hearts full of celestial melodies and dreams.

62

The Dance of the Fireflies

Luna and Iris encounter a magical forest where fireflies illuminate the night with a mesmerizing dance, teaching them the beauty of living in the present.

Once upon a time, in a tranquil forest aglow with the gentle light of the moon, Luna and Iris found themselves wandering through a magical grove. A symphony of lights danced through the night, illuminating the forest in a celestial spectacle. Fireflies, like living stars, moved in graceful harmony.

Enchanted by this radiant ballet, Luna and Iris watched the fireflies weave their luminous tapestry in the velvety night. Each delicate movement was a piece of a greater, more profound dance. The pair sat down amidst the shimmering display, humbled and mesmerized by the beauty that enveloped them.

The fireflies continued their performance, each one seemingly aware of its role in this cosmic dance. Their synchronized movements painted ephemeral constellations in the dark expanse, and a feeling of serenity washed over Luna and Iris. It was a living, breathing symphony that sang of the purest moments in life: the present.

With the fireflies as their guides, Luna and Iris learned a valuable lesson about the beauty of living in the moment. The past and future lost their grip as they embraced the here and now. A sense of awe filled their hearts as they realized the profound gift of presence.

The forest became a sanctuary of serenity, where time seemed to stand still. Luna and Iris joined the dance, allowing themselves to become a part of the glowing, ever-shifting tapestry. In the company of these marvelous creatures, they discovered the joy of simply being.

As the night unfolded, Luna and Iris took away a precious memory, etching this ethereal experience into their hearts. They now understood that life was a lot like the fireflies' dance: it was about the moments that illuminated our journey and made it magical.

With a newfound appreciation for the gift of the present, Luna and Iris continued on their adventures, knowing that the dance of the fireflies would forever remind them of the beauty of living in the moment.

63

The Whispers of the Forest

Luna and Iris explore an ancient forest and learn about the importance of conservation and connecting with nature.

Once upon a time, in a world of dreams and possibilities, there lived a curious and adventurous cat named Luna and her friend Iris. Luna was not an ordinary cat—she had a heart that yearned for exploration and a spirit that longed for new experiences.

One day, Luna and Iris found themselves standing at the edge of a lush and ancient forest. The trees towered overhead, their branches creating a canopy that filtered the sunlight into a gentle, dappled dance of shadows and rays. The forest seemed to beckon them in with its mellow whispers and secrets.

With every step they took into the forest, the air became fresher, the earthy scent of moss and fallen leaves filling their senses. Luna and Iris felt a deep connection to the vibrant life surrounding them. They saw squirrels leaping from branch to branch, birds singing their sweet melodies, and the occasional glimpse of a shy deer among the trees.

As they ventured deeper into the forest, the duo couldn't help but notice the gentle harmony of life within. It was as if every creature, every plant, had a role in the symphony of nature. The forest had its rhythm and heartbeat and sang a soothing, timeless song.

Luna paused to observe the wildflowers that lined their path. She bent down to take in their fragrance. "Iris, these flowers are exquisite. They seem to be whispering to each other."

Iris nodded in agreement. "It's as if the whole forest is in conversation. They're reminding us of the importance of preserving and nurturing this delicate balance of life."

Their journey led them to a majestic ancient oak tree with gnarled roots that seemed to burrow deep into the earth's core. Luna touched the tree's rough bark, feeling the wisdom and strength that emanated from it.

"This tree has seen centuries pass," Luna whispered, awestruck.

Iris placed her hand beside Luna's, feeling the energy of the tree as well. "Indeed. It's a testament to the resilience and timelessness of nature. It also reminds us of our responsibility to protect these places."

They sat under the ancient oak, contemplating the wisdom they had gained. They knew they needed to share the lessons from the forest with others. The importance of conservation, the interconnectedness of all living beings, and the beauty of nature's delicate harmony were lessons they carried in their hearts.

As they left the forest, they did so with a promise to be stewards of the natural world, to cherish its beauty, and to share the whispers of the forest with those willing to listen.

64
The Lost Lullaby

Luna and Iris venture into a realm of forgotten dreams and help a lost lullaby find its way back to a child's heart.

One day, in a realm between dreams and reality, Luna and Iris found themselves surrounded by a tranquil, silvery mist. As they wandered deeper into this mysterious place, the soft echoes of a gentle melody reached their ears. The melody was a lullaby that seemed to carry the weight of forgotten memories and unspoken wishes.

The source of the melody remained hidden until Luna and Iris noticed a faint, shimmering light ahead. As they drew nearer, the light resolved into the form of a small radiant star-child. The star-child was bathed in a gentle, ethereal glow and cradled a luminous lullaby in his tiny arms.

The star-child looked at Luna and Iris with sparkling eyes and an aura of innocence. With a voice as soft as the petals of a sleeping rose, he whispered, "I am the guardian of this lost lullaby, left here in this realm of dreams. It yearns to find its way back to a child's heart, but it has become trapped, entangled in the web of forgotten memories and abandoned dreams."

Luna and Iris exchanged glances, understanding the importance of the task before them. With a graceful nod, they expressed their willingness to help. As Luna stretched out her hand, the lullaby floated gently into her palm. It was a fragile, shimmering thing, like gossamer threads woven from moonlight and stardust.

Guided by the star-child, they embarked on a journey through the dream realm, a place where forgotten dreams scattered like stardust and unspoken wishes twinkled like distant constellations. Luna and Iris ventured deep into the heart of this realm, where they encountered dreamscapes that were both hauntingly beautiful and hauntingly sad.

They met a dreamer who had lost her way and forgotten her purpose. With their gentle guidance, they whispered to the dreamer, encouraging her to believe in herself once more. In the soft moments of dawn, they watched as a faint smile spread across her face, rekindling her belief in the magic of dreams.

In another dream, they discovered a wish that had been abandoned. It was a wish to heal a wounded heart locked away in the darkest corners of the dreamer's mind. Luna and Iris nurtured the desire with empathy and understanding until it was strong enough to shine again.

Through their compassion, Luna and Iris weaved a tapestry of hopes and dreams, each repaired and revitalized. With every step, the lullaby in Luna's hand pulsed with renewed vigor, its melodies growing more intricate and beautiful.

The journey was not without its challenges. Luna and Iris faced dream-weavers who sought to unravel their progress and return the lullaby to the realm of forgotten dreams. But with unwavering determination and the power of empathy, they overcame these obstacles.

At last, the radiant star-child led them back to the realm where they had first arrived. With a twinkle in the eye, the star-child whispered a heartfelt thank you, and the lullaby began to resonate with a heartwarming tune. As the lullaby's notes blended harmoniously with Luna and Iris's voices, they felt the collective power of dreams, wishes, and memories.

The lost lullaby was ready to find its way back to the child's heart from which it had been separated for so long. Luna held it aloft, and the ethereal light surrounding the lullaby expanded, forming a glowing path that reached far into the dream realm. The path meandered through the dreams of countless dreamers, illuminating forgotten wishes and rekindling hope.

Luna and Iris released the lullaby with a whispered promise to visit the realm of dreams again. It followed the path of light, weaving through the tapestry of dreams, returning to the child who had once held it in their heart.

As Luna and Iris watched the lullaby's journey, they knew they shared something extraordinary. Their hearts swelled with the knowledge that, in the realm of dreams, they had helped mend the connections between forgotten dreams, unspoken wishes, and the hearts of dreamers.

With a sense of fulfillment, Luna and Iris returned to their realm, carrying the warmth and magic of the dream world with them. The memories of their journey would forever echo in their hearts, reminding them of the beauty of dreams and the importance of keeping them alive.

65

The Harmony of the Humpbacks

Luna and Iris join a pod of humpback whales as they sing their songs across the vast oceans, emphasizing the importance of embracing diversity.

Once upon a time, in a world of dreams and possibilities, there lived a curious and adventurous cat named Luna and her friend Iris. Luna was not an ordinary cat—she had a heart that yearned for exploration and a spirit that longed for new experiences.

Luna and Iris stood at the water's edge, staring out at the vast expanse of the ocean. It was a clear, sunny day, and the waves lapped gently at the shore. The distant cries of seagulls added to the tranquil atmosphere, and the air was filled with the salty scent of the sea.

As Luna and Iris took in the beauty of the ocean, they noticed a disturbance on the horizon. A group of humpback whales breached the surface, their massive bodies curving gracefully through the water. The whales leaped into the air, their tails crashing down with a resounding splash. Luna and Iris watched in awe as the whales seemed to be dancing, their songs filling the air with a haunting melody.

"Wow, look at them, Iris," Luna said, her voice filled with wonder. "They're like the ocean's own symphony. They're like a testament to the beauty and diversity of life beneath the waves."

Iris nodded in agreement. "It's incredible, Luna. I had read about humpback whales and their songs, but I never imagined we'd witness this first hand."

The two friends sat down on the sandy beach with their eyes fixed on the mesmerizing display. The whales sang in unison, creating a harmony that resonated deeply within Luna and Iris. The music seemed to speak of ancient stories of migrations across vast oceans and the bonds that tied the pod together.

But as Luna and Iris listened, they noticed something else about the whales. Some were larger, while others were smaller. Their songs varied in pitch and tone. The differences among the humpbacks were evident, but it was these variations that made their collective song so beautiful and unique.

"Iris," Luna said, "it's as if the whales are telling us a story about the importance of diversity, about embracing our differences and finding strength in our unity."

Iris smiled, her eyes sparkling with understanding. "Yes, Luna. Just like the whales, we each have our unique qualities and talents. When we come together and celebrate our differences, then we create something truly harmonious and beautiful."

As the sun began to set, Luna and Iris continued to listen to the humpback whales' song, their hearts filled with gratitude for this extraordinary moment by the sea. They knew that the harmony they'd witnessed would stay with them, a reminder of the beauty of diversity and the power of unity.

Luna and Iris made their way back to the cottage, carrying with them the profound wisdom of the humpback whales. They knew that they were part of a vast world, rich with diverse life and that their journey was far from over. With each new adventure, they would continue to learn, grow, and be inspired by the wonders of the universe.

66

The Starry Night Adventure

Luna and Iris travel to a world where the night sky reveals the aspirations of people from different cultures and backgrounds as a canvas of dreams.

One day, Luna and Iris found themselves in a place unlike any they had ever seen. The sky above them was alive with a mesmerizing display of stars, each one twinkling and sparkling like a tiny beacon of hope. The two friends looked up in awe, their eyes wide with wonder.

As they continued to gaze at the starry spectacle, Luna noticed that the stars formed intricate patterns, like a celestial puzzle. "I've heard of constellations," Luna said, "but I've never seen them so vividly."

Iris, always curious, fluttered up to get a closer look. "These constellations seem to tell a story," she mused. "Each one is a piece of the cosmic puzzle, a glimpse into the dreams and aspirations of people from different cultures and backgrounds."

Luna nodded in agreement. "It's like the universe is trying to tell us something, Iris."

The two friends decided to embark on a journey through this enchanting starry landscape. As they ventured deeper into the night sky, they encountered a series of constellations, each more beautiful and intriguing than the last.

They stumbled upon "The Dreamer's Lyre." Luna touched one of the stars, and it emitted a soft, melodic tune. "This must be the dream of a musician," Luna said. "Creating such beautiful music that resonates with the soul."

Iris found "The Explorer's Compass." "Someone dreamed of discovering new worlds, of endless adventure and exploration," Iris observed. "How exciting!"

Their journey led them to "The Painter's Palette." Luna and Iris could almost smell the fresh paint and feel the artist's inspiration. "This person dreamt of filling the world with beauty through their art," Luna said with admiration.

As they continued their celestial exploration, they discovered countless more constellations, each representing a different dream or aspiration. Their adventure had shown them that dreams were as vast and varied as the stars themselves. They marveled at the diversity of human aspirations and the importance of dreams in shaping the world.

Luna and Iris returned to their world with hearts full of inspiration and gratitude. They knew that the dreams and aspirations they had encountered in the starry night would continue to guide and inspire them on their adventures.

67

The Garden of Compassion

Luna and Iris discover a garden where each flower represents an act of kindness, teaching them the transformative power of compassion.

Luna and Iris awoke one sunny morning, feeling a sense of excitement in the air. The two friends could tell that something special was waiting for them just around the corner.

They noticed a low, melodic hum in the distance as they made their way through the forest. Following the sweet sound, they soon arrived at the entrance of a garden. But this was no ordinary garden—it was the Garden of Compassion.

The moment Luna and Iris stepped inside, they were greeted by an array of vibrant, blooming flowers. Each flower was unique, with colors and shapes that Luna and Iris had never seen before.

"What makes this garden so extraordinary?" Luna wondered aloud.

Before Iris could respond, the flowers began to speak. It wasn't a spoken language, but a communication that touched the heart and soul.

The flowers shared their stories, and Luna and Iris felt a profound connection. Each flower represented an act of kindness, compassion, or love that someone had shown to another. The garden was filled with the energy of these beautiful acts.

Luna and Iris approached a radiant sunflower. It told the story of a little girl who had gifted a bouquet of sunflowers to her grandmother, bringing her joy and warmth. The energy of this act had blossomed into this sunflower's life.

Next, they spoke to a delicate orchid, which shared the story of a stranger who had helped a lost traveler find their way. The energy of this act had infused the orchid's very existence with grace and elegance.

In this garden, kindness and compassion were the seeds that brought the flowers to life. Acts of love and support, both big and small, had given each bloom its unique beauty.

As they walked through the garden, Luna and Iris couldn't help but think about the power of compassion and its impact on the world. They realized that even the simplest acts of kindness could have profound effects, like the flowers in the garden.

With grateful hearts, Luna and Iris decided to leave their own mark of kindness. They planted a new flower, and as they watered it with love and care, they knew its beauty would continue to grow and spread throughout the world. Leaving the Garden of Compassion, Luna and Iris felt inspired. They now understood the transformative power of kindness and compassion, knowing that even the littlest acts could make the world a more beautiful place.

The two friends left the garden with hearts full of compassion and a mission to carry this message into the world. As they journeyed forward, they carried the beauty of the Garden of Compassion in their hearts, sharing kindness and warmth wherever they went.

68

The Symphony of Seasons

Luna and Iris embark on a journey through a land where every season is a different symphony of colors, emphasizing the beauty of change and transition.

Once upon a time, in the cozy town of Everwood, nestled at the edge of a vast, enchanted forest, there lived two inseparable friends, Luna, the curious blue cat, and Iris, the graceful butterfly.

On a sunny morning, Luna and Iris decided to venture deeper into the enchanted forest, where whispers of wonders beyond imagination beckoned them. They felt the air grow crisper and the fragrance of pine and earth filled their senses with each step.

As they journeyed further, the trees around them began to change. Luna noticed the leaves transition from shades of vibrant green to warm hues of orange, red, and yellow. "Iris," Luna said, "Do you hear that? It's like the forest is singing!"

Iris fluttered around Luna's head, her wings a symphony of color. "You're right, Luna. It's as if the forest is alive with music. I think it's welcoming us to a new season."

Indeed, the forest seemed to be singing the symphony of autumn. Leaves danced gracefully, falling to the ground like the notes of a melodious tune. The duo wandered through the carpet of leaves, the soft rustling creating the sweetest lullaby.

They continued their exploration, and with every step, the world around them changed. The clear blue sky transformed into a canvas of frosty blues and whites. The melody of winter was upon them as icicles dangled like chimes, glistening in the pale sunlight. Luna and Iris found themselves captivated by the delicate frost patterns that only nature could create.

Then came spring, and the forest was alive with the joyful chorus of birds. Luna and Iris found themselves in a sea of wildflowers, their vibrant colors a testament to the season's vitality. The world around them seemed to burst with life, and the forest whispered tales of rebirth.

Finally, summer arrived, and the forest was in full bloom. Luna and Iris watched as the trees donned a rich coat of green and the air buzzed with the hum of cicadas. They discovered a crystal-clear stream, and as they dipped their paws and wings into the cool water, they felt like they were part of this living symphony.

Luna looked at Iris with wonder in her eyes. "Every season has its music, and it's a reminder that change can be beautiful."

Iris nodded, her wings shimmering in the dappled sunlight. "Yes, Luna. Just as the forest transitions through its seasons, so do our lives. Change brings new experiences and beauty."

As they made their way back to Everwood, the forest seemed to bid them farewell with a grand finale of colors and melodies, celebrating the ever-turning wheel of time.

69

The Flight of the Monarchs

Luna and Iris follow the path of migrating monarch butterflies, learning about the courage it takes to follow one's own path.

One day, Luna and Iris found themselves in a meadow bursting with vibrant wildflowers. The colors were so mesmerizing that it seemed like the world itself had turned into a magnificent garden. But what truly stole their attention were the graceful monarch butterflies fluttering in a delicate dance above the blossoms.

As Luna and Iris observed these splendid creatures, they noticed that the butterflies had gathered near a grove of trees. It was as if the monarchs had a secret of their own that was waiting to be revealed.

Intrigued, Luna and Iris followed the flight of the monarchs as they gently navigated the cool breeze. The butterflies moved with a sense of purpose, weaving between the trees like the living petals of a swirling flower.

As the duo ventured deeper into the grove, they found something truly enchanting. Hanging from the branches of the trees were countless cocoons, each a delicate and intricate masterpiece. Luna and Iris understood that these cocoons held the pupae of the monarch butterflies, soon to be reborn and continue the circle of life.

Suddenly, they heard a soft, melodic whisper in the wind. It was the voice of the butterflies, imparting their wisdom. The monarchs revealed that they undertook an incredible journey—the migration from faraway lands to reach this meadow. They spoke of their remarkable ability to navigate thousands of miles, guided solely by the whispers of the wind.

Luna and Iris were filled with awe and wonder. They asked the butterflies how they could embark on such a daring adventure, and the butterflies replied, "Courage lies within the heart of every living being. To follow your path is to discover the beauty of your transformation."

The butterflies' message resonated deeply with Luna and Iris. They realized that, like the monarchs, they, too, could have the courage to follow their dreams and navigate life's vast and unknown journeys. The whispers of the wind carried with them a powerful truth: the heart knows the way.

With newfound inspiration, Luna and Iris continued their journey. As they left the meadow, they felt the gentle caress of the wind whispering their names and guiding them forward.

Their adventure with the monarch butterflies had left a profound impression. Luna and Iris had learned that courage could guide them to explore the boundless horizons of their dreams.

70

The Secret Language of Trees

Luna and Iris stumble upon an ancient forest with trees that communicate through vibrations. They discover the importance of interconnectedness and shared knowledge.

Once upon a time, in a world of dreams and possibilities, there lived a curious and adventurous cat named Luna and her friend Iris. Luna was not an ordinary cat—she had a heart that yearned for exploration and a spirit that longed for new experiences.

One day, Luna and Iris found themselves wandering deeper into the enchanted forest. Ancient trees with intertwined roots formed a canopy so thick that it seemed like dusk even though the sun was high in the sky. Birds of every color and shape adorned the branches, singing sweet songs.

But Luna and Iris soon noticed that it wasn't only the birds making music. The trees themselves seemed to hum with life. They watched as the leaves shivered in harmony, and the trunks emitted low, resonant notes.

Curiosity led them to a wise old oak tree. Its bark was weathered, and it appeared to have witnessed countless seasons. Luna and Iris felt a pull, a soft, rhythmic vibration. They extended their hands and placed them on the tree's rough surface.

The moment they touched the tree, they felt a surge of energy. Suddenly, they could understand the language of the forest.

The oak tree whispered, "I am centuries old, and I've seen the world change. I've spoken to countless creatures, but humans seldom listen."

Luna and Iris were captivated. "What is the secret language of trees?" Iris asked.

The oak tree began to explain, "Each species of tree communicates in its unique way. We share our stories from ancient times when the world was young. We tell of seasons and life cycles and of the balance that all creatures must respect."

Luna inquired, "Can we learn this language?"

The oak tree nodded, "Of course, but it's not through spoken words; it's through feeling. To understand our language, you must open your hearts and senses, for it is the language of the soul."

So, Luna and Iris began to listen, not with their ears but with their souls. They felt the life force surging through the forest. The mighty oak spoke of strength and wisdom, the willow of flexibility and resilience, and the maple of transformation.

As they listened to the trees' whispers, they realized the interconnectedness of the forest. The roots communicated beneath the earth, providing mutual support, and the leaves collected the wisdom of the wind.

Over time, Luna and Iris grew skilled in the secret language of the trees. They learned to speak not with words but with their hearts and formed a lifelong bond with the ancient forest.

Their newfound connection with the trees showed them the importance of listening, not just with their ears but with their hearts and souls. It was a reminder that nature had many lessons to offer if one was willing to pause and listen.

71

The Marvelous Metropolis

Luna and Iris visit a magical city where the buildings come to life at night. They learn about the importance of imagination and creativity in shaping the world around us.

One day, Luna and Iris, our adventurous feline and butterfly duo, found themselves in a city where the buildings had a life of their own. During the day, the city seemed like any other, but as the sun dipped below the horizon and the moon graced the sky, the metropolis transformed into a spectacle of colors and stories.

As the two friends strolled along the cobblestone streets, they noticed the buildings slowly waking up and stretching out their windows like yawning creatures waking from a deep sleep. The great clock tower in the city center chimed, setting off a harmonious symphony that resonated through every brick and stone. The skyscrapers began to shimmer with vibrant hues, casting a magnificent display that painted the night sky.

Curious as always, Luna and Iris approached one of the structures, an old library with wise and welcoming eyes. The building opened its doors, revealing an enchanting interior filled with towering shelves of books. The walls whispered forgotten tales, and the wooden floor hummed with the echoes of stories from long ago. The duo couldn't resist the temptation and entered, ready for another marvelous adventure.

Inside, they met the Bookmaster, a kind and wise figure who held the keys to countless stories. The Bookmaster explained that the city was a place where imagination and creativity were celebrated. Each building had a unique story, and each night, they came alive to share their narratives with those willing to listen.

Luna and Iris roamed from building to building, discovering a bakery that kneaded stories into loaves of bread and a theater where characters from the pages of history danced on the stage. They visited a music conservatory where melodies floated through the air like fireflies and an art gallery where paintings shifted and morphed to tell stories.

Through their magical journey in the marvelous metropolis, Luna and Iris learned that creativity and imagination were the heartbeats of this world. They realized that every person, like the buildings of the city, had their own unique stories to tell and were woven into the fabric of the world's larger narrative.

As the sun's first rays began to touch the horizon, the metropolis started to return to its slumber. The buildings, one by one, closed their doors and settled back into their daytime façades. Luna and Iris said their goodbyes to the marvelous city, knowing that they carried a piece of its magic within their hearts.

With the lessons of creativity, imagination, and the power of stories, our two adventurous friends continued their journey, eagerly awaiting the next wonder they would encounter.

72

The Garden of Dreamful Wonders

Luna and Iris stumble upon a hidden garden where dreams grow as colorful flowers. They discover the significance of nurturing our dreams and turning them into reality.

Once upon a time, in a world where dreams had a life of their own, Luna and Iris found themselves on a journey to a hidden and magical place known as the Garden of Dreamful Wonders.

The garden was a well-kept secret, tucked away behind a veil of secrecy within the heart of the Enchanted Forest. Luna and Iris, with their curious spirits, embarked on this adventure, guided by whispers carried by the wind. It had been said that the garden is a place where dreams grow into colorful flowers, waiting to be nurtured and come true.

As Luna and Iris ventured deeper into the Enchanted Forest, they encountered a peculiar path. The trees seemed to lean in and beckon them forward, casting dappled shadows on the ground. The intoxicating scent of blossoming dreams filled the air.

They followed the path, and with each step the world changed around them. The forest became alive with an array of vibrant colors and an energy they had never experienced before. Gigantic butterflies danced in the air, and whimsical fireflies created a luminous tapestry overhead.

Finally, they arrived at the Garden of Dreamful Wonders. It was a sight to behold. Dreams had taken on various forms, each more beautiful than the last. There were dreams of friendship, dreams of adventures, dreams of love, and dreams of exploring the world.

The garden was tended by a wise and gentle gardener, a being whose wisdom was as vast and deep as the ocean. She explained to Luna and Iris that dreams need to be cared for and nurtured like the most delicate of flowers.

She showed them how to water their dreams with determination and how to nurture them with patience. The imagination requires love, belief, and effort to grow and bloom into reality. And so, Luna and Iris began tending their dreams in the garden. They learned that the Garden of Dreamful Wonders held the power to make dreams come true.

After much care and nurturing Luna and Iris watched in awe as their dreams began to take root and sprout. As their imaginations grew, they took on vibrant colors, just as the flowers in the garden did. It was a testament to the power of imagination, belief, and hard work.

With hearts full of gratitude, Luna and Iris knew that dreams were not just figments of the imagination. They were the seeds of a beautiful and fulfilling life. They returned to their world, taking with them the invaluable lesson that dreams could become a reality if they were cared for and nurtured.

The Garden of Dreamful Wonders had shown them that life is full of magical opportunities waiting to be embraced. The garden whispered, "Dream big, believe, and tend to your dreams like you would the most precious of flowers, and you'll discover a life full of wonder."

Luna and Iris returned to their world with hearts full of dreams and determination to turn them into reality, knowing that with patience, belief, and hard work, they could make their dreams bloom like the flowers in the Garden of Dreamful Wonders.

73
The Stars of Unity

Luna and Iris travel to the night sky and meet the constellations, each with its unique story. They learn about diversity and how working together creates something truly beautiful.

One day, Luna and Iris embarked on a celestial journey guided by the luminous stars that punctuated the vast night sky. The moonlight painted a silvery path, leading them deeper into the heavens. As they ascended, a sense of wonder embraced them.

Among the stars, Luna and Iris met a constellation known as "The Weaver." The Weaver was an intricate network of stars, shining brightly and interconnecting to form a beautiful, ever-evolving pattern. Luna and Iris were mesmerized by the dazzling display, their eyes tracing the connections.

"Each star in this constellation," explained the Weaver, "represents a unique story, a life lived, and a purpose fulfilled. Together, they create something greater than the sum of their parts."

Luna and Iris continued their celestial journey and encountered another constellation named "The Musician." This constellation sparkled with stars arranged in the shape of musical notes, and it resonated with sweet melodies that filled the cosmos.

"I embody harmony," the Musician explained. "Just as each note has its place and significance in a composition, every individual brings their unique gifts to the world. It's in the symphony of unity that true beauty emerges."

As their journey continued, Luna and Iris marveled at the constellation "The Painter." It was a vivid cluster of stars arranged in the form of a vast canvas with vibrant colors and intricate strokes.

"The Painter's message," it shared, "is that every stroke, every hue, and every detail contributes to the masterpiece of life. Diversity in thought, expression, and experience is what creates the richness of our world."

The night sky was filled with countless other constellations, each with its own story of unity and diversity. Luna and Iris left this celestial realm with hearts filled with hope, realizing that just as the stars shone brightest together, humans could achieve greatness through unity in diversity.

They returned to earth, knowing that their journey was enriched by the lessons of the stars. Every being, like a star, had a unique place in the constellation of life, contributing to the beauty of the world when united.

74

The Enchanted Library

Luna and Iris find a library filled with books that allow them to experience the stories firsthand. They learn about empathy, the power of storytelling, and how to put themselves in someone else's shoes.

Once upon a time, in a quiet corner of the town of Serendipity, Luna and Iris stumbled upon a mysterious library. As they stepped through the threshold, they were transported into a world where the stories in books came to life. The shelves were lined with countless tales, each one more enchanting than the last.

Luna and Iris were astounded as they witnessed classic tales like *Cinderella*, *Alice in Wonderland*, and *Robin Hood* unfolding before their eyes. They could join Cinderella at the royal ball, shrink down like Alice and explore the wonderland, or join Robin Hood in his quest for justice.

What made this library truly magical was its ability to instill empathy in those who read its stories. Luna and Iris found themselves not only watching but also experiencing the lives of the characters. They laughed with them, cried with them, and learned from them. It was a unique form of storytelling that allowed them to step into someone else's shoes.

In one corner, they met a young boy named Oliver Twist, who taught them about resilience and the importance of helping others. In another, they sailed the high seas with the daring Captain Nemo, gaining a deeper appreciation for the oceans and marine life.

They discovered that every story had a valuable lesson to offer, and the more stories they experienced, the more empathetic and understanding they became. It was as though the library was a portal to the hearts and minds of countless individuals from different times and places.

As Luna and Iris spent days exploring the library, they realized that the power of storytelling was immense. It could bridge gaps, foster understanding, and bring people closer together. They vowed to share this newfound knowledge with the people of Serendipity and beyond so that everyone could experience the enchanting world of empathy through the magic of stories.

And so, Luna and Iris continued their adventure, knowing that the library had not only enriched their own lives but had given them a gift to share with the world: the gift of empathy, one story at a time.

75

The Symphony of Silence

Luna and Iris enter a world where silence has a unique voice, teaching them about mindfulness and the beauty of finding peace within.

One day, Luna and Iris found themselves in a place where silence spoke volumes. The air was still, and the world seemed to hold its breath as if savoring the peaceful moment.

As they explored this unique world, they realized that in silence, they could hear the whispers of nature. The gentle rustle of leaves, the distant babble of a brook, and the soft hum of a bumblebee became a part of their symphony. It was a world where mindfulness reigned, and every moment held significance.

Luna and Iris decided to sit down under a grand old tree. With eyes closed, they listened to the silence, their breathing slowing and their minds calming. The sensation was like being cradled in a cocoon.

In the stillness, they heard the song of the wind, a gentle lullaby that seemed to be soothing the earth itself. They realized that silence had a unique voice, one that whispered truths only the heart could understand.

As they continued to explore, they stumbled upon a field of wildflowers. The flowers stood tall and proud, their vibrant colors seemingly brighter in the hush of this realm. Luna and Iris felt a profound connection to the flowers. Each petal, each leaf, and each stem was an expression of nature's gracc.

The pair found a tranquil pond, its surface like a mirror reflecting the azure sky above. They watched as a dragonfly floated above the water, creating ripples that spread outward. Luna and Iris saw in this simple act the beauty of interconnectedness, how every action had a consequence, and how everything in the world was connected in the grand symphony of life.

At sunset, as they sat by the pond, the first stars began to twinkle in the night sky. The celestial bodies seemed to communicate in silence, each with its own story. Luna and Iris contemplated the vastness of the universe, realizing that sometimes the most profound connections were made without words.

The Symphony of Silence had taught Luna and Iris the importance of mindfulness, of being fully present in the moment. They discovered that in the quietest moments, the world spoke volumes, and the beauty of life was often found in stillness.

As they left this unique world, they carried with them a newfound appreciation for silence, a deeper connection to nature, and the knowledge that within the symphony of life, silence played a profound and beautiful part.

76
The Ocean's Dance

Luna and Iris take a dive into the ocean, meeting marine creatures who perform an underwater ballet. They learn about the balance and harmony in nature.

One day, Luna and Iris, their hearts brimming with excitement, embarked on an unforgettable journey to the coast. The cerulean ocean stretched before them, its crystal-clear waters inviting them to dive into its secrets. With a deep breath and a sense of adventure, they submerged themselves in the marine world.

As they descended into the depths, the ocean unveiled its dazzling treasures. A burst of colors greeted their eyes. Schools of fish, each more brilliant than the last, moved in perfect unison, creating a captivating spectacle of motion. It was as if they were engaged in an underwater ballet, moving with the precision and grace of world-class dancers. A group of seahorses wove through the water, their tails forming intricate patterns as they twirled.

The enchanting dance of the marine creatures seemed orchestrated. Graceful sea turtles swayed majestically while dolphins leaped in joyful acrobatics, adding music and rhythm to the mesmerizing ballet.

Finn, a friendly clownfish, welcomed Luna and Iris to this underwater wonderland. He explained that every creature in the ocean played a unique role, contributing to the delicate balance and harmony of their aquatic realm. The seahorses transported nutrients and upheld the ecosystem's web of life. The sea turtles nurtured the seagrass beds, providing vital shelter for countless marine species. The dolphins, with their boundless energy, shared their infectious spirit and laughter.

Luna and Iris swam alongside these incredible creatures, learning their secrets and joining in their dance. They marveled at the collaboration, unity, and understanding that existed in this underwater world. Each motion and gesture was a part of nature's silent symphony, a language that transcended words.

Emerging from the ocean, Luna and Iris felt like they were leaving a realm of pure magic. The lessons they carried with them were profound. They understood that nature had its unique ways of communicating, but they could tune in to its rhythms. The oceans taught them about the importance of balance, unity, and collaboration in the natural world.

Looking out over the vast expanse of the ocean from the shore, Luna and Iris gazed at its beauty with a newfound appreciation. It was a living masterpiece, a symphony of silence. It was a testament to the intricate relationships that bound the earth's ecosystems together.

As they headed home, their hearts were filled with gratitude. The wisdom of the ocean's dance would forever resonate within them, a reminder of the interconnectedness and harmony that could be found in every corner of the world.

77

The Doorway to Time

Luna and Iris come across a mysterious doorway that lets them visit different time periods. They discover the importance of history and how it shapes our future.

Once upon a time, in a world of dreams and possibilities, there lived a curious and adventurous cat named Luna and her friend Iris. Luna was not an ordinary cat—she had a heart that yearned for exploration and a spirit that longed for new experiences.

Luna and Iris were walking through the enchanted forest when they stumbled upon a peculiar stone archway covered in intricate vines and glowing with an otherworldly light. Curiosity got the best of them, and they stepped through the archway, not knowing what to expect.

As they passed through, they found themselves transported to a different time, surrounded by ancient architecture and an unfamiliar landscape. Luna looked down at her feet and saw that the ground was not the grassy forest floor they had left behind but a cobblestone street.

The ever-curious explorer, Luna, jumped onto a nearby stone ledge and peered down into a bustling marketplace. They had traveled back in time to a vivid and bustling medieval city, complete with merchants haggling over the price of goods, street performers entertaining the crowd, and the aroma of fresh-baked bread wafting through the air.

Luna and Iris marveled at the cobblestone streets, the towering cathedral, and the intricate architecture that surrounded them. They walked through the market square and saw knights in shining armor, minstrels playing cheerful tunes, and townsfolk going about their daily routines.

They then passed through the arch once more and found themselves in another era. And this time they were standing in a quaint Victorian garden. Iris noticed children in elegant clothing playing with old-fashioned toys. The air was filled with the melody of a violin played by a musician in the corner and the sweet smell of roses.

The magical archway transported Luna and Iris through different eras of history. It also gave them a unique opportunity to witness the beauty and diversity of the human experience throughout time. With each visit, they gained a deeper understanding of how history had shaped the world and influenced the people living in those times.

Upon their return to the present, Luna and Iris felt a newfound appreciation for history and the importance of preserving it. They realized that the lessons of the past could guide humanity to a brighter future, teaching them about the consequences of their actions and the value of preserving the beauty and culture of their own time.

As they stepped away from the archway, they knew that their adventure through time had imparted a timeless lesson. They were ready to face the present with a greater understanding of history and an eagerness to shape a better future.

78

The Artistry of the Elements

Luna and Iris enter a realm where they can communicate with the elements—earth, water, air, and fire. They learn about the importance of respecting and preserving the natural world.

Once upon a time, in a world of dreams and possibilities, there lived a curious and adventurous cat named Luna and her friend Iris. Luna was not an ordinary cat—she had a heart that yearned for exploration and a spirit that longed for new experiences.

In the heart of a mystical forest, Luna and Iris embarked on a journey that would connect them to the very essence of the world. A hidden grove, untouched by time, awaited them. In this sacred place, the elements thrived, each with its unique personality, and Luna and Iris were about to become a part of their world.

As the duo ventured deeper into the grove, the symphony of nature enveloped them. The towering oaks whispered ancient secrets to the wind. Rivers revealed stories etched into the very earth they caressed. Luna and Iris felt the warmth of the fire's spirit and the cool embrace of the water's presence. The air that surrounded them carried the wisdom of the ages, and they realized they had entered a realm where the elements were truly alive.

In a tranquil clearing, where dappled sunlight danced through the leaves, Luna and Iris encountered the spirits of the elements. Each spoke in a voice that resonated within their very souls.

"I am Earth," the gnarled tree spoke, its voice a comforting murmur. "I am the silent observer, the patient creator. My strength lies in nurturing and grounding all life."

Iris, enticed by the glistening stream, dipped her fingers into the water, and it rippled with joy. "I am Water," the voice chimed, a melody of fluidity. "Ever adaptable, I am life-giving and cleansing. I weave tales of emotion and connection."

A gentle gust of wind swirled around them, carrying a whisper of wisdom. "I am Air," it sighed, a voice of gentle encouragement. "I am the breath of life, the messenger of change. I bring the power of communication and the songs of flight."

The warmth of the sun bathed Luna and Iris, and they felt the presence of a flickering spirit. "I am Fire," it crackled, the spark of enthusiasm. "I am the spark of creation and transformation. My passion ignites courage and fuels the fires of innovation."

The elements continued to share their stories with Luna and Iris, revealing the intricate balance of life. Together, they painted a picture of harmony, an interconnected dance that sustained the circle of existence. It was a dance that spoke of unity, of preserving the sanctity of nature's delicate balance.

Luna and Iris left the grove with the wisdom of the Earth, Water, Air, and Fire etched into their souls. They carried with them the realization that each element was a guardian of the earth, contributing to the beautiful tapestry of existence in its unique way.

As they ventured back into the world, they held a deeper understanding of the artistry of the elements, a profound respect for the delicate balance of nature, and a shared commitment to preserving the natural world. The elements had woven their magic, and Luna and Iris were now part of a timeless masterpiece.

79

The Kingdom of Colors

Luna and Iris find themselves in a world where color is magic. They learn about the significance of diversity, tolerance, and celebrating differences.

Once upon a time, in a world of dreams and possibilities, there lived a curious and adventurous cat named Luna and her friend Iris. Luna was not an ordinary cat—she had a heart that yearned for exploration and a spirit that longed for new experiences.

Luna and Iris embarked on a journey that transported them to the Kingdom of Colors, a place where color was tangible magic. As they stepped into this realm, they were greeted by a landscape painted in vibrant hues. The trees had leaves in shades never seen on earth, and the skies shifted from one mesmerizing color to another.

Luna and Iris were greeted by the Color Guardians, the stewards of this magical land. Each Guardian were dedicated to one specific color, representing the essence of that hue. The kingdom was a place where the magic of diversity, tolerance, and the celebration of differences flourishes.

The Color Guardians explained that the uniqueness of this kingdom was in the way it valued every shade and hue. In their world, it was not just about acceptance, but a whole hearted appreciation of what each color brings to the collective canvas. They understood that the beauty of their kingdom was a result of the harmonious blend of all colors. Just as in our world, diversity and inclusion enrich our communities.

As Luna and Iris journeyed through the Kingdom of Colors, they noticed that the inhabitants of this realm were multiple colors, signifying their ability to understand and embody various perspectives. Others were dedicated to the arts, using their creativity to mix colors and create astonishing pieces that told stories of unity, compassion, and acceptance.

Throughout their adventure, Luna and Iris witnessed incredible displays of cooperation, harmony, and love. They saw how this colorful world celebrated the strengths and attributes of each individual, knowing that it's the synergy of their differences that made the kingdom extraordinary.

The Kingdom of Colors taught Luna and Iris that celebrating differences, being open to various perspectives, and nurturing the magic of diversity is the key to a world filled with love, respect, and unity. They returned to their world with a profound understanding that diversity is our strength and that every color, be it in our personalities or appearances, is a unique brushstroke contributing to the magnificent painting of life.

80

The Mystery of the Melody Maker

Luna and Iris encounter a creature with the power to create music by dancing. They learn about the importance of finding joy in creativity and self-expression.

One day, Luna and Iris found themselves in a realm of vibrant colors and surreal landscapes where flowers sang and the rivers whispered secrets. The very air was alive with an otherworldly energy. They ventured deeper into this enchanting world, their curiosity guiding their path.

As they continued their journey, they were drawn to a clearing illuminated by a soft, iridescent glow. In the center of the clearing stood a remarkable being, its body adorned with shimmering scales that seemed to shift through every color of existence. The creature stood tall on two legs; its slender form poised with an air of grace.

The moment the Melody Maker moved, its presence was felt in the radiant notes that trailed behind it. Each step the Melody Maker took left a trail of glistening musical notes that hung in the air like a tapestry of a sound. They sparkled like stardust, and Luna and Iris watched in awe as the ethereal notes danced around them.

The creature extended a delicate hand towards them, inviting them to join in a celestial dance. Without hesitation, Luna and Iris approached the Melody Maker. As they began to dance, they discovered that their every movement created harmonious notes that intertwined with those of the Melody Maker.

As they danced, their movements became a form of self-expression. The music they created was not bound by words or instruments; it was a language of the heart, conveying emotions that words could never capture. The Melody Maker's music was more than only sound; it was an enchanting melody that resonated deep within the soul.

As Luna and Iris twirled and leaped to the rhythm of the dance, they felt their own emotions weave into the melodies. Joy, sadness, love, and wonder all became part of the symphony they created. It was as if they could express their deepest feelings without saying a word.

The Melody Maker, with a voice like the wind through a forest, spoke to their hearts. It explained that creativity and self-expression were powerful forms of magic that resided within every living being. The dance was a testament to the idea that each person, creature, or even a leaf rustling in the wind could create something beautiful.

The music that they created had the power to touch hearts, forge connections between souls, and inspire others to express their unique voices. It wasn't about being the best dancer or the most skilled musician; it was about the act of creation itself. Their dance was a celebration of the pure, unadulterated joy of self-expression.

As the sun sank below the horizon, Luna and Iris knew their time with Melody Maker was coming to an end. They stopped their dance, their breathless laughter hanging in the air. They thanked the Melody Maker for the priceless lesson it had bestowed upon them: the profound significance of creativity and self-expression.

With hearts full of gratitude and memories of the enchanting music, they left the vivid realm and continued their journey. The music of the Melody Maker echoed within them, a melody they would carry throughout their adventures.

81

The Enchanted Mirror

Luna and Iris discover a magical mirror that shows them the beauty within, teaching them the importance of self-acceptance.

One day, in the heart of the enchanting forest, Luna and Iris made an astonishing discovery. Hidden amidst the ancient trees and the whispers of the wind, they stumbled upon a magnificent mirror. Its ornate frame, adorned with exquisite carvings of mythical creatures, and its ethereal, glowing glass hinted at its extraordinary nature.

Luna and Iris gazed at the mirror in wonder, their eyes filled with curiosity. As they looked into it, they noticed something incredible. It was no ordinary mirror; it possessed a magical quality. The reflection that stared back at them wasn't just a mere image of their physical appearance. It went much deeper, revealing the essence of their very beings.

Iris was the first to see it. Her reflection in the mirror showed not only her outward appearance, but also the kindness in her eyes, the compassion in her heart, and the boundless love for those around her. Luna, too, saw beyond her physical form. In the mirror's gaze, she recognized the courage that allowed her to face any challenge, the creativity that sparked her boundless curiosity, and the unwavering spirit that drove her to explore the unknown.

The mirror seemed to understand them in a way that no one else ever had. It recognized their unique qualities and talents, emphasizing their inner beauty and self-worth. Luna and Iris stood there, enchanted and astounded, realizing that this mirror had the power to reveal the beauty within a person.

For hours, they remained in front of the mirror, engrossed in their reflections. It was as if the mirror had unlocked a hidden treasure within their souls, revealing qualities and virtues they had never fully appreciated before. Iris saw her kindness, a strength that made her unique and truly special. Luna recognized her creativity, which was the wellspring of her boundless curiosity and exploration.

What was most astonishing was that the mirror seemed to respond to their self-acceptance and self-love. As Luna and Iris looked within themselves and recognized their worth, the mirror's glow intensified. It was as if the more they appreciated their beauty, the brighter the mirror shone.

Leaving the enchanted mirror behind, Luna and Iris felt transformed. They understood a profound lesson—the magic of self-acceptance and self-love. They now knew that every person possessed unique qualities and virtues that made them special, irreplaceable, and truly beautiful. Recognizing and cherishing these inner qualities was the key to unlocking the mirror's magic.

As Luna and Iris continued their journey, they carried this invaluable lesson with them. They were now equipped with the power of self-acceptance, an understanding that acknowledging one's inner beauty was the gateway to recognizing the beauty in others.

Throughout their travels, Luna and Iris shared their wisdom with those they encountered. They encouraged self-love and acceptance, teaching others to look within, recognize their unique qualities, and cherish the beauty that resides in their hearts. The enchanted mirror had given them a gift beyond measure: the knowledge that self-acceptance was the foundation for building stronger, more compassionate connections with the world around them.

Their hearts brimming with gratitude for the mirror's magical lesson, Luna and Iris moved forward, eager to share the power of self-acceptance and help others discover their inner beauty.

82
The Whispering Winds

Luna and Iris follow a gentle breeze to a land where the wind itself communicates, sharing stories of unity and understanding.

Once upon a time, in a world of dreams and possibilities, there lived a curious and adventurous cat named Luna and her friend Iris. Luna was not an ordinary cat—she had a heart that yearned for exploration and a spirit that longed for new experiences.

One day, Luna and Iris embarked on a journey led by a gentle breeze. It carried them to a land where the wind communicated, sharing stories of unity and understanding. As they ventured deeper into this unique realm, the wind enveloped them, caressing their faces and whispering ancient tales into their ears.

The wind began to share its wisdom in a hushed tone, revealing stories of the unity that existed between all things. It told them about the interconnectedness of the world. How the breeze carried the fragrance of blooming flowers, how it danced through the leaves of trees, and how it whispered secrets across vast distances.

One particular story the wind shared was about a grand oak tree. This tree stood tall and proud, its branches spreading far and wide, providing shelter for countless creatures. The wind explained that the oak tree represented strength and protection, and its connection to all living beings illustrated the importance of community and support.

Luna and Iris were moved by the story and felt inspired to continue their journey with an even deeper understanding of unity They realized that just as the wind connected the entire world, every living being was part of a larger tapestry of life. Each one had a role to play; and together, they created harmony.

The wind guided them to a tranquil glen, where animals of all kinds gathered around a sparkling stream. They observed that a deer, a rabbit, and a fox shared the same space without fear or aggression. The wind whispered that this scene represented the peaceful coexistence of different species, emphasizing the beauty of diversity and unity in nature.

As Luna and Iris continued their journey, they noticed the delicate dance of butterflies and bees among the blossoms of wildflowers. The wind explained that these creatures relied on each other to thrive. The flowers provided nectar for the butterflies and bees, while the insects, in turn, helped pollinate the plants, ensuring the cycle of life continued.

In this enchanted land, Luna and Iris discovered that unity and understanding were not just principles; they were a way of life. The wind reminded them that they, too, were part of this grand tapestry. By embracing the lessons of the wind and cherishing the interconnectedness of all living things, they could contribute to the harmony of the world.

With this newfound wisdom, Luna and Iris set forth on the next leg of their journey, their hearts filled with gratitude for the gentle winds that had whispered stories of unity in their ears.

83
The Timeless Lighthouse

Luna and Iris visit a mystical lighthouse that can illuminate time, emphasizing the importance of guidance and perspective.

One day, Luna and Iris ventured towards a secluded, enchanting beach guided by a distant, flickering light. As they approached, the source of the radiant beacon became clear—a magnificent lighthouse stood tall and strong against the elements.

The lighthouse cast light on the sea, but also appeared to illuminate the past, present, and future. A warm, inviting glow wrapped around the structure, revealing stories etched into the stones and whispers of adventures long gone.

Entranced by this extraordinary sight, Luna and Iris stepped inside the lighthouse. The air was thick with the scent of salt and history. Inside, they found a vast, spiraling library of light, where shelves of radiant books glowed with the knowledge of centuries.

They reached out to one of the books and as their fingers touched its cover, a rush of memories and visions washed over them. Luna was transported to the days of ancient mariners navigating the treacherous waves by the lighthouse's guiding light. Iris saw a glimpse of the present—a family enjoying a picnic on the same beach, their laughter echoing in the distance. And then, they glimpsed a future where the lighthouse stood as a beacon of hope, its light guiding generations yet to come.

A wise, ethereal presence materialized before them, a spectral keeper of the lighthouse. “Welcome, young travelers,” it whispered, “I am the guardian of time’s light. This lighthouse illuminates not only the sea but the stories of those who have been here and those who are yet to come. Time is a river, and the lighthouse is a bridge between its shores.”

Luna and Iris were humbled and filled with curiosity. “Why are you showing us all this?” Luna asked.

“Because,” the guardian replied, “the lighthouse seeks to teach you the importance of guidance and perspective. Just as it lights the way for ships at sea, wisdom and insight can guide your path through life. To understand where you’re going, you must know where you’ve been and be open to what the future holds. The lighthouse serves as a reminder that time is a precious, ever-flowing river, and each moment is a drop in the vast ocean of existence.”

With newfound appreciation, Luna and Iris thanked the guardian for the lessons and the beauty of the lighthouse. They left the enchanted beach, carrying with them the lighthouse’s wisdom and the understanding that the journey of life is not just about the destination but the illumination of the path along the way.

As they walked back into the world, they felt more connected to the past, present, and future, knowing that their journey was a part of a grander narrative. The lighthouse’s light was not just a beacon for sailors; it was a beacon for their souls, reminding them of the timeless beauty and wisdom to be found in every moment.

84
The Library of Dreams

Luna and Iris return to the enchanted library, but this time, the books they read come to life, allowing them to explore the dreams and aspirations of people from various cultures.

One day, Luna and Iris found themselves in front of the gorgeous, enchanted library once again. The ornate doors beckoned them inside, and as they stepped through, a sense of wonder washed over them.

The library bathed in a warm, golden light, and the soft rustle of pages filled the air. This time, however, something was different. As Luna and Iris wandered deeper into the library's labyrinthine corridors, they noticed that the books seemed to shimmer with a subtle magic.

Curiosity sparked in their eyes, and they reached for a book that radiated a soft, inviting glow. As Luna opened the cover, they were enveloped in a swirl of colors and transported to another world. They found themselves in a bustling market in a far-off land.

The air was filled with bright colors and the enticing aroma of exotic spices. People from various cultures moved gracefully through the market, each one with a unique story to tell. Luna and Iris realized that the book had brought to life the dreams and aspirations of the people within its pages.

They met a young musician who played melodies that touched the soul of everyone who listened. His dream was to spread the joy of music to all corners of the world. Luna and Iris watched as he shared his music with the people, and they felt the power of his dream.

Further on, they encountered a wise elder who held a book filled with ancient knowledge. Her dream was to preserve the wisdom of her ancestors and pass it on to future generations. Luna and Iris listened to her stories, learning valuable lessons about history and the importance of cherishing one's heritage.

In yet another book, they met a passionate chef who dreamt of uniting people through the magic of food. Luna and Iris savored the delicious dishes she prepared, feeling the bonds of community and togetherness.

With each book they opened, Luna and Iris continued to explore the dreams and aspirations of people from different cultures and backgrounds. They realized that dreams had the power to connect people, no matter how far apart they were or how different their lives might seem.

As they closed the final book, Luna and Iris found themselves back in the enchanted library. The books now seemed to glow even more brightly, and the shelves were filled with countless untold dreams, waiting for someone to discover and share them.

The magical experience left Luna and Iris with a profound sense of gratitude for the diversity of dreams and aspirations. They understood that dreams were the threads that wove the tapestry of our shared humanity. The library had shown them that no dream was too small, no aspiration too insignificant, and that each one contributed to the beauty of the world.

With newfound inspiration, Luna and Iris left the library, ready to chase their own dreams and inspire others to do the same. As they stepped back into the world, they carried with them the precious knowledge that dreams had the power to unite, illuminate, and create a more beautiful and connected world.

85

The Seeds of Hope

Luna and Iris find a secret garden filled with seeds that, when planted, grow into beautiful, resilient flowers, teaching them the power of hope and transformation.

Once upon a time, in a world of dreams and possibilities, there lived a curious and adventurous cat named Luna and her friend Iris. Luna was not an ordinary cat—she had a heart that yearned for exploration and a spirit that longed for new experiences.

In the heart of a hidden forest, Luna and Iris stumbled upon a hidden garden bathed in the soft glow of sunlight filtering through the leaves. The ground beneath their feet felt like a carpet of moss, and the air was filled with the delicate scent of blooming flowers.

As Luna and Iris explored the garden, they noticed something extraordinary—seeds of various shapes and sizes scattered throughout the lush landscape. Curiosity sparked in their eyes as they approached the seeds, wondering about their origin and purpose.

Suddenly, a gentle breeze whispered through the branches and a soft voice echoed in the air, "Welcome, seekers of hope. These are the Seeds of Hope, planted by the dreams and wishes of those who have sought solace in this magical garden."

Intrigued, Luna and Iris decided to plant a seed themselves. As they gently placed it in the fertile soil, a burst of energy emanated from the ground. The seed began to sprout, unfurling delicate green leaves that reached for the sunlight. It transformed into a radiant flower, its petals painted in vibrant hues.

The garden came alive with colors, each flower representing a story of resilience, courage, and dreams fulfilled. Luna and Iris soon realized that the Seeds of Hope held the power to transform despair into beauty and adversity into strength.

As they continued to explore, they encountered a wise old tree in the center of the garden. Its branches stretched high, adorned with blossoms that shimmered like stars. The tree spoke, "Dear travelers, the Seeds of Hope teach us that even in the darkest times, the potential for growth and beauty exists. Every challenge is an opportunity for transformation."

Luna and Iris were filled with a profound sense of gratitude and hope. They understood that just as the seeds flourished in the garden, they, too, could nurture hope in their hearts and sow the seeds of positive change in the world around them.

With newfound inspiration, Luna and Iris left the secret garden, carrying the wisdom of the Seeds of Hope with them. They knew that wherever they went, they could plant seeds of kindness, compassion, and optimism, contributing to the beauty and resilience of the world. A reminder that hope, once planted, could bloom into a garden of endless possibilities.

86

The Riddles of the Sphinx

Luna and Iris travel to a place where they must solve riddles to progress, learning about critical thinking and the value of wisdom.

Once upon a time, in a world of dreams and possibilities, there lived a curious and adventurous cat named Luna and her friend Iris. Luna was not an ordinary cat—she had a heart that yearned for exploration and a spirit that longed for new experiences.

One day, in the heart of an enigmatic realm, Luna and Iris found themselves surrounded by ancient structures and towering statues, the atmosphere steeped in mystery. The air resonated with otherworldly energy, and the gentle breeze carried whispers of riddles that waited to be unraveled. Standing before them was the Sphinx, a majestic creature with the body of a lion and the head of a wise human.

The Sphinx, regal and all-knowing, extended a welcoming nod and presented the first riddle: "I speak without a mouth and hear without ears. I have nobody, but I come alive with the wind. What am I?"

Luna and Iris exchanged glances, a spark of curiosity in their eyes. The Sphinx observed with a knowing smile, accustomed to witnessing the attempts of countless travelers to decipher the secrets of the land.

After a thoughtful pause, Luna ventured her answer, "An echo!"

The Sphinx's eyes gleamed with approval and as a reward, a hidden passage opened before them, leading them deeper into the captivating realm of riddles. Each step forward met with new challenges, not just in the form of intellectual puzzles but also as tests of their collaborative spirit and creative thinking.

As they progressed, Luna and Iris realized that the answers to the riddles were not mere solutions but gateways to profound insights. The Sphinx, through its cryptic questions, became a guide, steering them toward a greater understanding of perspective, imagination, and the interconnectedness of knowledge.

Their journey was not without its trials. Some riddles appeared insurmountable initially, but Luna and Iris grew to appreciate the process of exploration and the joy of unraveling mysteries one layer at a time. The Sphinx, a silent witness to their journey, watched with satisfaction as they absorbed the lessons hidden within each enigma.

Reaching the heart of the land, the Sphinx posed a final riddle that resonated with deep wisdom: "I am always hungry, always need to eat. The finger I lick will soon be red. What am I?"

Luna and Iris shared determined glances, recognizing that this riddle held the key to completing their quest. After a moment of intense contemplation, Iris smiled and confidently responded, "It's fire!"

The Sphinx applauded their success, and the land around them shimmered with a warm, golden light. They had not only unraveled the riddles but also gained a profound understanding of the value of knowledge, curiosity, and the timeless pursuit of wisdom.

With hearts filled with gratitude, Luna and Iris bid farewell to the Sphinx, carrying the lessons with them as they continued their extraordinary journey through the realms of wonder.

87
The Song of Serenity

Luna and Iris enter a world where music is more than just sound; it's a way of healing and fostering inner peace.

One day, Luna and Iris found themselves standing at the edge of a lush meadow, the air filled with a gentle melody that seemed to resonate from the very flowers and trees that surrounded them. As they ventured further into this musical realm, the source of the enchanting sound revealed itself.

In the heart of the meadow stood a majestic tree, its branches swaying in harmony with the breeze. Each leaf on the tree seemed to carry a note, creating a symphony that resonated with the colors of the flowers beneath it. Luna and Iris were captivated by the beauty of this living melody.

Curious, they approached the tree, and as they did, the music seemed to respond to their presence. The tree's branches rustled and began to form intricate patterns in the air, each movement creating a new layer of the melody. It was as if the tree could communicate through its music.

As Luna and Iris continued their exploration, they discovered that every element in this magical land was attuned to the language of music. The babbling brook hummed a soothing tune, and the butterflies fluttered in rhythmic patterns. Even the sunlight filtering through the leaves seemed to play a part in the grand composition.

Guided by the music, Luna and Iris felt a profound sense of peace and serenity wash over them. It was as if the harmonious notes had the power to heal and uplift their spirits. They understood that in this world, music was not just a form of entertainment but a language that could touch the soul and bring about a sense of inner calm.

As the day unfolded, Luna and Iris found themselves joining in the dance of the music. They swirled around the meadow, their laughter blending seamlessly with the symphony of nature. It was a moment of pure joy, a celebration of the magical connection between music and the soul.

As the sun began to set in a warm glow over the meadow, Luna and Iris knew they had experienced something truly special. The song of serenity had left an indelible mark on their hearts, reminding them of the healing power that resides in the language of music.

With gratitude and a newfound sense of tranquility, Luna and Iris bid farewell to the musical realm, carrying the song of serenity with them on their continued journey through the enchanting lands that awaited.

88

The Circus of Imagination

Luna and Iris join a circus where the performers bring their wildest dreams to life, encouraging them to embrace their imagination and creativity.

Once upon a time, in the enchanting world where Luna and Iris roamed freely, a new spectacle awaited them: a circus. As Luna and Iris approached the colorful tent that seemed to stretch into the heavens, the air buzzed with anticipation.

Upon entering, they were greeted by the vibrant hues of the circus tents and the tantalizing scent of cotton candy lingering in the air. The performers, adorned in dazzling costumes, moved gracefully to the rhythm of an invisible melody. Luna and Iris couldn't help but be captivated by the magical atmosphere.

As they explored further, they discovered that this circus was unlike any other. It wasn't just about acrobats, jugglers, and clowns; it was a realm where dreams transformed into reality. The performers were dream-weavers, and the tent itself was a portal to the limitless landscapes of the imagination.

The first act unveiled before Luna and Iris was a breathtaking display of flying elephants with wings made of rainbows. The majestic creatures soared through the air, leaving trails of sparkling stardust behind them. Luna and Iris watched in awe as the performers demonstrated the boundless possibilities that could unfold when one dared to dream.

In the other corner of the circus, a carousel with creatures of myth and legend—unicorns, griffins, and phoenixes—rotated. The music played by an ethereal orchestra echoed through the tent, creating a harmonious symphony that resonated with the beating hearts of all who witnessed it.

The ringleader, a wise old owl perched on a high wire, called Luna and Iris to join the spectacle. With a twinkle in his eye, he explained, "Here, in the Circus of Imagination, every dream has a place. Embrace the extraordinary and let your imagination soar."

Luna and Iris hesitated for a moment, unsure of what to contribute to such an extraordinary gathering. But then, inspired by the kaleidoscope of wonders around them, they closed their eyes and let their minds wander.

And just like that, the world around them transformed. Luna found herself riding a comet, trailing stardust as she soared through galaxies, while Iris danced with constellations, each step leaving a burst of light in the cosmic tapestry.

The crowd erupted in cheers, celebrating the arrival of new dreams into their whimsical realm. The Circus of Imagination showcased the limitless potential residing within the human spirit—a celebration of creativity, courage, and the beautiful tapestry woven by the dreams of every individual.

As Luna and Iris took their bows, the ringleader nodded approvingly. "Remember," he whispered, "the circus is always here, waiting for dreamers like you to join the grand spectacle of imagination."

With that, Luna and Iris left the tent, their hearts brimming with newfound inspiration and a deeper understanding of the magic that dwells within the boundless landscapes of imagination.

89

The Enchanted Moonlit Forest

Luna and Iris venture into a mystical forest that comes to life under the light of the full moon. They discover ancient secrets, magical creatures, and the beauty of nature's nocturnal wonders.

Once upon a time, in a world of dreams and possibilities, there lived a curious and adventurous cat named Luna and her friend Iris. Luna was not an ordinary cat—she had a heart that yearned for exploration and a spirit that longed for new experiences.

One day, Luna and Iris strolled hand in hand into the heart of the Enchanted Moonlit Forest. The tall and wise trees seemed to whisper ancient tales as the duo ventured further. The moon, a radiant orb in the velvety sky, cast a silvery glow upon the surroundings, bringing the mystical forest to life.

As Luna and Iris stepped beneath the moon's enchanting light, the flora and fauna responded with a symphony of color and sound. Flowers of every hue bloomed, releasing fragrances that danced in the cool night air. The creatures of the forest, both magical and mundane, began to awaken, welcoming the two explorers with curious gazes.

The full moon acted as a guide, illuminating a path that led deeper into the heart of the woodland. Along the way, Luna and Iris encountered ancient trees, their trunks adorned with glowing runes that told stories of times long past. Each step felt like a journey through history as if the forest itself held the memories of ages gone by.

As they ventured further, Luna and Iris discovered a clearing bathed in moonlight. In the center was a crystal-clear pool, reflecting the celestial glow above. The surface of the water seemed to ripple with the energy of the enchanted forest. Luna and Iris approached the pool, their reflections joining the myriad images of the moonlit surroundings.

Suddenly, a soft melody filled the air as if played by invisible musicians. The duo looked around, trying to discern the source of the enchanting tune. To their surprise, the very leaves of the trees seemed to rustle in harmony, creating a celestial song that resonated with the magic of the moonlit night.

As Luna and Iris listened, they felt a connection to the ancient rhythm of the forest. The enchanted flora and fauna are communicated through the language of music, conveying tales of resilience, transformation, and the enduring beauty of nature's nocturnal wonders. It was a symphony of life, a dance of existence, and Luna and Iris found themselves swaying to the ethereal melody.

In that moment, surrounded by the moonlit magic of the Enchanted Forest, Luna and Iris understood the interconnectedness of all living things. The ancient secrets whispered by the trees, the fragrant blossoms, and the celestial melody were a testament to the enduring power of nature and the profound beauty that unfolded beneath the gentle gaze of the moon.

With hearts filled with gratitude, Luna and Iris continued their journey through the Enchanted Moonlit Forest, guided by the celestial glow that painted the night with wonder.

90

The Whispers of the Breezes

Luna and Iris embark on an adventure where they can communicate with the wind. They learn to understand the secrets carried by the breezes and the importance of listening to nature's whispers.

Once upon a time, in a world of dreams and possibilities, there lived a curious and adventurous cat named Luna and her friend Iris. Luna was not an ordinary cat—she had a heart that yearned for exploration and a spirit that longed for new experiences.

One day, Luna and Iris found themselves in a meadow bathed in golden sunlight. The air was filled with the delicate scent of wildflowers, and the gentle rustle of leaves hinted at the magic awaiting them. As they stood hand in hand, a soft breeze began to weave its way around them, carrying with it the secrets of the meadow.

The breeze, a whimsical guide, invited Luna and Iris to close their eyes and open their hearts to the language of the wind. With a gentle touch, the wind whispered tales of distant lands, ancient trees, and the dance of seasons. Each breath of air was a story, a melody that painted vivid images in the minds of our two adventurers.

Luna, her eyes closed, felt the breeze playfully tousling her hair. She sensed the wind's gentle laughter as if it held the secrets of a thousand joyous moments. Iris, too, embraced the whispers of the breezes, feeling a connection to the very pulse of nature.

The wind carried them across the meadow, where they discovered a hidden grove. As they stepped into the heart of the grove, the whispers intensified. The trees seemed to share their wisdom, telling stories of growth, resilience, and the beauty of transformation.

Luna and Iris learned that, just like the wind, life was a continuous journey of change. Seasons may shift, leaves may fall, and yet, new buds emerge, promising a tapestry of colors yet unseen. The secrets of the breezes revealed the interconnectedness of all living things and the importance of embracing the ebb and flow of existence.

In this enchanted grove, Luna and Iris discovered their ability to communicate with the wind. They found that by listening, truly listening, they could understand the language of nature. The breezes taught them the importance of stillness, of being present in the moment, and of allowing the whispers of the world to guide them on their journey.

Luna and Iris left the grove hand in hand as the sun dipped below the horizon, their hearts filled with the wisdom carried by the breeze. The wind, now a constant companion, continued to share its tales as they ventured into the next chapter of their extraordinary adventure.

91

The Enchanted Starlight Grove

Luna and Iris discover a hidden grove where the stars come to rest during the day. They learn about the interconnectedness of all things and the importance of finding moments of tranquility.

Once upon a time, in a world of dreams and possibilities, there lived a curious and adventurous cat named Luna and her friend Iris. Luna was not an ordinary cat—she had a heart that yearned for exploration and a spirit that longed for new experiences.

In a land where magic and wonder flourished, Luna and Iris stumbled upon a hidden gem, a place known only to a few—the Enchanted Starlight Grove. This mystical sanctuary revealed its secrets as the radiant sun rose above the horizon, allowing the stars to descend and rest among the ancient trees.

As Luna and Iris entered the grove, they were greeted by a soft, ethereal glow. It was as if the stars themselves had transformed into tiny fireflies, casting a gentle light that painted the surroundings with a celestial palette. The air was filled with the sweet melody of night, and the ground sparkled with the reflections of a thousand starry companions.

Amidst the ancient trees stood a wise old figure, a celestial guardian who watched over the grove. The guardian, a luminous being made of stardust and dreams, welcomed Luna and Iris with a nod that echoed the rustling leaves in the breeze.

"Welcome, wanderers," the celestial guardian spoke, his voice a melodic blend of whispers from distant galaxies. "Here in the Enchanted Starlight Grove, the stars find solace and rejuvenation. Just as they rest, so too can you find tranquility and connection in this sacred place."

Luna and Iris were drawn deeper into the grove, their senses heightened by the magical energy that enveloped them. Each step seemed to synchronize with the heartbeat of the universe. They created a dance of harmony between the celestial and the earthly.

The guardian shared the wisdom of the grove, teaching Luna and Iris about the interconnectedness of all things. He spoke of the delicate balance between the heavens above and the world below. And emphasized the importance of finding moments of calm and reflection in the ever-turning wheel of time.

As the night unfolded, Luna and Iris felt a profound sense of unity with the cosmos. They learned that, just like the stars, they were part of a vast and intricate tapestry, each thread contributing to the whole. The grove whispered tales of cosmic connections, ancient as time itself; stories of love, resilience, and the eternal dance between light and darkness.

With gratitude in their hearts, Luna and Iris bid farewell to the Enchanted Starlight Grove, carrying with them the radiant energy of the stars. As they stepped back into the realm of the everyday, they knew that the magic of the grove would forever be a guiding light in their journey.

And so, under the canvas of the night sky, Luna and Iris continued their adventure, their spirits illuminated by the wisdom of the Enchanted Starlight Grove.

92

The Puzzle of Reflections

Luna and Iris encounter a mysterious pond that reflects the inner thoughts and emotions of those who gaze into it. They discover the power of self-awareness and understanding.

One day, in a picturesque forest, where sunlight filtered through the leaves like golden rain, Luna and Iris stumbled upon a serene clearing. This haven, adorned with vibrant flowers and ancient trees, exuded an otherworldly charm. As the duo ventured deeper, a mysterious pond, its surface as smooth as glass, unveiled itself.

Captivated by the pond's mystical aura, Luna and Iris approached with a mixture of excitement and reverence. To their astonishment, the moment they gazed into its tranquil waters, the surface transformed into a mesmerizing display of colors and images. It was as if the pond held the power to reveal the deepest reflections of one's inner self.

Intrigued and eager to unravel the secrets of this enchanted pond, Luna and Iris spent hours observing its magical manifestations. The pond, it seemed, held the collective consciousness of the entire forest. If a butterfly fluttered by, its joyous dance reflected on the water. When a gentle breeze whispered through the leaves, the pond echoed the soft rustle of the foliage.

As Luna and Iris observed, they realized that the pond not only mirrored their thoughts and emotions but also those of the creatures and plants around them. It became a living tapestry of the interconnectedness of all living things.

Curiosity evolved into a thirst for understanding, Luna and Iris decided to delve deeper into the puzzle of reflections. They experimented with the intentions behind their gaze, discovering that the pond responded to the purity of their emotions. If their hearts resonated with joy and gratitude, the pond painted scenes of happiness and harmony. However, if any shadows of doubt or fear lingered, the reflections mirrored those uncertainties.

This interactive dance with the pond became a transformative experience for Luna and Iris. They realized that the key to deciphering the puzzle lay in the clarity of one's thoughts and the purity of one's intentions. The pond, in its mystical wisdom, encouraged self-awareness and understanding.

With newfound insights, Luna and Iris continued their exploration of the enchanted forest. The pond, now a cherished memory, continued to ripple with the reflections of countless tales from those who dared to gaze into its depths.

And so, the journey of Luna and Iris unfolded, filled with the magic of self-discovery and the profound wisdom found in the reflections of the heart. Each ripple on the pond's surface became a reminder of the interconnected dance of life, where every thought and emotion contributed to the ever-unfolding tapestry of existence.

93

The Symphony of Dreams

Luna and Iris enter a realm where dreams take on a tangible form. They learn about the significance of aspirations, imagination, and the pursuit of one's goals.

One day, in the heart of a celestial realm, Luna and Iris found themselves surrounded by an ethereal glow. It was a place where dreams transcended the boundaries of sleep, taking on vivid, tangible forms that danced in the air like graceful butterflies.

The Symphony of Dreams played out before Luna and Iris as a mesmerizing orchestra of colors and shapes. Each note resonated with aspirations, weaving a tapestry of imagination that stretched across the horizon. Luna, with her shimmering fur, and Iris, with her vibrant wings, felt an immediate connection to this enchanting symphony.

As they ventured deeper into this dream-infused domain, they encountered dream-weavers—mystical beings responsible for crafting the very fabric of these fantastical visions. Through their gentle whispers, these beings shared stories of individuals whose dreams had become reality, leaving inspiration for others to follow.

The first form Luna and Iris encountered was that of a towering tree, its branches reaching toward the sky with an unwavering determination. a dream-weaver revealed that this tree embodied the dream of growth, symbolizing the resilience and strength required to overcome challenges.

Moving forward, Luna and Iris encountered a river of flowing stardust, its currents guiding them through a dreamscape painted with constellations. A dream-weaver explained that this cosmic river represented the journey of self-discovery and the pursuit of knowledge—an endless quest for understanding the mysteries of the universe.

Continuing their exploration, Luna and Iris came across a city of floating islands, each holding the dreams of a thriving community. A dream-weaver narrated tales of collaboration, unity, and the collective pursuit of shared aspirations, emphasizing the power of dreams to create bonds that transcend individual ambitions.

The Symphony of Dreams unfolded like a kaleidoscope, presenting an endless array of forms, each telling a unique story. Luna and Iris, entranced by the magic around them, absorbed the wisdom of the dream-weavers and the dreamscape itself.

As they prepared to leave this ethereal realm, Luna and Iris carried with them the harmonious melodies of the Symphony of Dreams. They understood that dreams were not just ephemeral illusions but powerful forces capable of shaping destinies. With hearts filled with inspiration, Luna and Iris soared back to their reality, eager to share the tales and lessons they had gathered in the realm where dreams took flight.

94

The Lullaby of the Moon

Luna and Iris befriend a celestial creature that creates a soothing lullaby with the phases of the moon. They discover the calming influence of nature and the importance of rest.

Once upon a time, in the heart of the Moonlit Meadow, Luna and Iris returned to the hidden grove where the stars found repose during the day. As they ventured deeper into the grove, a celestial creature named Serena emerged—a gentle being adorned with the ethereal glow of the moon.

Serena, the guardian of the moon's phases, welcomed Luna and Iris with a soothing lullaby that resonated through the celestial expanse. The friends were captivated by the melody and as they listened, Serena extended an invitation: "Come, dear ones, let me be your guide through the wondrous dance of the moon."

Under the shroud of the new moon, where the sky embraced velvety darkness, Serena's lullaby spoke of new beginnings, of how it was a blank canvas of possibilities. At the heart of the grove, Luna and Iris felt the canvas of possibilities stretch before them. It was a time of introspection, setting intentions, and sowing the seeds of aspirations.

With the emergence of the waxing crescent, a slender silver sliver in the night sky, Serena's lullaby echoed themes of anticipation. Luna and Iris learned to nurture their dreams, for the waxing crescent symbolized the gradual illumination of aspirations. It was a phase of inspiration, a time to embark on their journeys of self-discovery.

In the first quarter, when the moon revealed half of its radiant face, Serena's lullaby guided Luna and Iris through the delicate dance of balance. It was a reminder to harmonize their energies, balancing action with reflection. Serena's celestial symphony became a teacher, revealing the importance of finding stability amidst life's fluctuations.

The moon waxed toward its full brilliance, and Serena's lullaby carried a crescendo of energy. Luna and Iris understood that this phase was a time of manifestation. Intentions, sown during the new moon, now sprouted into tangible realities. The waxing gibbous became a celebration of growth and the materialization of dreams.

When the moon reached its full splendor, bathing the world in silver radiance, Serena's lullaby reached its zenith. Luna and Iris felt a surge of energy and illumination. The full moon unveiled hidden truths and brought clarity to their hearts. It was a time of culmination and acknowledgment—a cosmic celebration of achievements and revelations.

The waning descent began, and Serena's lullaby took on a gentler tone. Luna and Iris learned that the waning gibbous phase was a time of reflection. It encouraged them to express gratitude for their experiences and release anything that no longer served them. Serena's celestial melodies guided them through the gentle process of letting go.

In the last quarter, with half of the moon's face veiled in shadow, Serena's lullaby conveyed the beauty of transitions. Luna and Iris understood that transitions were inherent in the cosmic dance of life. The last quarter became a time of acceptance and preparation for the upcoming renewal cycle.

The moon waned toward the new moon, and Serena's lullaby whispered of the beauty in stillness. Luna and Iris discovered the power of rest and introspection during the waning crescent phase. It was a time to recharge, reassess, and prepare for the next cycle of the moon's enchanting dance.

Beneath the celestial canopy of Moonlit Meadow, Luna and Iris continued their journey, accompanied by the timeless rhythms of Serena's lullaby. The melody echoed the cyclical dance of the cosmos and the interconnectedness of all things.

95
The Whispering Willows

Luna and Iris explore a magical forest where the willow trees communicate through gentle whispers. They learn about the strength found in compassion and empathy.

One day, in the heart of the Enchanted Forest, Luna and Iris found themselves surrounded by tall, graceful trees adorned with shimmering leaves that seemed to glisten with ancient secrets. Among these, the willow trees stood out, their long, cascading branches reaching toward the forest floor.

A soft murmur filled the air as Luna and Iris entered the forest. The willow trees were alive with whispers, each gentle rustle of their leaves carrying a message. The air was filled with a soothing melody, a symphony of nature's communication.

Intrigued, Luna and Iris approached one of the majestic willow trees. Its branches seemed to bend in a welcoming gesture, inviting the two friends to listen closely. As they leaned in, the whispers became words, and the words wove tales of compassion and empathy.

The willow shared stories of its long life, witnessing the joys and sorrows of the creatures that called the Enchanted Forest home. Luna and Iris learned about the interconnectedness of the forest, how every rustle of leaves, every sigh of the wind, held the echoes of the emotions shared by its inhabitants.

Guided by the gentle whispers, Luna and Iris ventured deeper into the magical grove. They discovered that the willow trees could empathize with the creatures around them. When a woodland creature felt joy, the willows swayed in celebration. In times of sorrow, their branches offered comforting whispers.

As Luna and Iris continued their exploration, they encountered various animals, each with a story to tell. The deer spoke of unity among the forest dwellers while the wise owl shared insights into the importance of understanding one another. The playful squirrels giggled as they leaped from branch to branch, emphasizing the joy found in simple acts.

The Whispering Willows taught Luna and Iris that compassion was the lifeblood of the Enchanted Forest. Each creature, from the smallest insect to the towering willow trees, played a unique role in maintaining the delicate balance of the forest.

With newfound wisdom, Luna and Iris embraced the lessons of empathy and compassion. As they left the magical grove, the willow trees continued their gentle whispers, sending the two friends on their way with the harmonious melody of the Enchanted Forest echoing in their hearts.

96

The Dance of the Stardust

Luna and Iris witness a celestial dance as stardust comes to life. They discover the beauty in fleeting moments and the importance of cherishing the present.

Once upon a time, in a world of dreams and possibilities, there lived a curious and adventurous cat named Luna and her friend Iris. Luna was not an ordinary cat—she had a heart that yearned for exploration and a spirit that longed for new experiences.

One day, in a realm beyond the veil of reality, where stardust sparkled like tiny diamonds, Luna and Iris found themselves standing in a celestial grove. The air shimmered with magic as stardust twirled and danced in the soft glow of a thousand stars. The cosmic ballet unfolded before their eyes, a mesmerizing display of light and motion.

As Luna and Iris observed, they noticed that each particle of stardust told a unique story—a story of fleeting moments that held the essence of beauty and wonder. The celestial dance was a reflection of the transient nature of time, a reminder that every moment, no matter how brief, was a precious gem in the tapestry of existence.

The Stardust Keeper, a gentle figure formed from the very essence of the dance, approached Luna and Iris. With a voice that echoed through the cosmos, the Stardust Keeper spoke, "Welcome, curious wanderers. In the dance of stardust, you witness the echoes of moments that pass in the blink of an eye. Each twirl, each glimmer is a memory woven into the fabric of the universe."

Luna and Iris were entranced, absorbing the wisdom of the Stardust Keeper. The celestial dance spoke of the importance of nurturing the present, as each passing moment carried a unique beauty that could never be repeated. It was a lesson in embracing the transience of time and finding joy in the transience.

The Stardust Keeper invited Luna and Iris to join the dance, encouraging them to become part of the cosmic choreography. As they moved, they felt a deep connection with the universe, a sense of oneness with the stars, and an understanding that they, too, were part of the ever-changing cosmic story.

Amid the celestial dance, Luna and Iris realized that life was a continuous interplay of moments, each contributing to the grand masterpiece of existence. They learned that embracing the present moment allowed them to appreciate the beauty of life in all its forms.

As the dance reached its crescendo, Luna and Iris felt a profound gratitude for the lessons of the Stardust Keeper. With a final, graceful spin, the celestial dance came to an end, and the stardust settled, leaving the grove in tranquil splendor.

The Stardust Keeper smiled at Luna and Iris, their eyes reflecting the entire cosmos. "Remember, dear ones, the dance of stardust is within you. Cherish each moment, for in doing so, you become a part of the eternal cosmic tapestry."

With these words, Luna and Iris left the celestial grove, their hearts filled with the wisdom of the cosmic dance. Stardust remained in their wake, a gentle reminder that every moment held the magic of the universe, waiting to be discovered and cherished.

And so, Luna and Iris continued their journey, carrying the enchantment of the celestial dance with them, eager to explore the wonders that lay ahead in the ever-unfolding story of their adventures.

97

The Mirror of Kindness

Luna and Iris encounter a mirror that reflects acts of kindness. They learn about the ripple effect of compassion and the transformative power of goodwill.

One day, in a land not so far away, Luna and Iris found themselves in a serene meadow surrounded by flowers of every imaginable color. The air was filled with the sweet scent of blossoms, and a gentle breeze carried the melodic whispers of nature.

As Luna and Iris strolled through the meadow, they noticed a peculiar-looking mirror standing alone at the edge. It was framed with vines and adorned with enchanting symbols. Intrigued, Luna and Iris approached the mirror, wondering about its purpose.

To their surprise, the moment they stood before it, the mirror began to shimmer, and its surface transformed into a reflection of the meadow. However, this was no ordinary reflection. Instead, it showed images of kind and compassionate acts happening around the world.

Luna and Iris watched in awe as the mirror revealed scenes of people helping one another, sharing smiles, and extending gestures of kindness. There were children helping elders, strangers offering assistance, and communities coming together to support those in need.

As Luna and Iris continued to gaze into the mirror, they noticed something extraordinary. Every act of kindness reflected in the mirror sent ripples across its surface, creating a beautiful kaleidoscope of colors and patterns. The more kindness they showed, the brighter and more vibrant the reflections became.

Curious and inspired, Luna and Iris decided to participate in this dance of kindness. They began by planting seeds of compassion in the meadow, helping creatures in need, and spreading warmth wherever they went. As they did, the mirror responded with a symphony of radiant hues.

The mirror taught Luna and Iris a valuable lesson: that kindness, no matter how small, has a ripple effect that touches the hearts of many. It showed them that a single act of compassion could create a chain reaction, inspiring others to spread love and goodwill.

With newfound understanding, Luna and Iris left the meadow, carrying the mirror's wisdom in their hearts. They continued their journey, eager to share the magic of kindness and contribute to the ever-expanding tapestry of compassion woven by people all around the world.

And so, as Luna and Iris ventured forward, the mirror continued to reflect the countless acts of kindness, reminding everyone who gazed into it of the transformative power of goodwill.

98

The Song of the Celestial Whales

Luna and Iris discover a magical ocean where celestial whales sing songs that resonate throughout the cosmos. They learn about the interconnectedness of all living beings and the universal language of harmony.

One day, Luna and Iris found themselves on the edge of a vast, sparkling ocean. The water shimmered with the light of a thousand stars, and gentle waves carried a melodious tune. They noticed majestic creatures rising from the depths—the celestial whales.

These whales were beings of cosmic beauty, and their bodies adorned with patterns that mirrored constellations. Luna and Iris marveled at the graceful dance of the whales, their voices resonating like celestial melodies.

The duo approached the water's edge, and, to their amazement, the celestial whales noticed them. With a gentle flick of their tails, the whales created ripples that formed a bridge, inviting Luna and Iris to join them in the heart of the magical ocean.

Luna and Iris felt a profound connection with these cosmic beings as they stepped onto the whale-made bridge. The whales communicated with vibrations that transcended the boundaries of language. It was a song that echoed through the interconnectedness of all living beings and the universal language of harmony.

In this celestial symphony, Luna and Iris sensed the stories of distant galaxies, the whispers of ancient trees, and the laughter of every creature that had ever existed. The whales' song carried the essence of the universe, a timeless melody that spoke to the very core of their beings.

The celestial whales invited Luna and Iris to join their harmonious dance. Together, they moved through the vast ocean, weaving patterns of light and sound that painted the sky with colors unseen by mortal eyes. Each movement of the whales created a cosmic masterpiece, a living tapestry of interconnected existence.

As the journey unfolded, Luna and Iris felt a profound sense of unity with the cosmos. They realized that, just like the celestial whales, every being played a unique role in the grand symphony of life. Each action, no matter how small, contributed to the ever-evolving melody of existence.

Eventually, as the celestial whales concluded their majestic dance, Luna and Iris found themselves back at the water's edge. The bridge of ripples dissolved, and the ocean returned to its calm, reflective state. The whales, their bodies aglow with celestial light, bowed gracefully before disappearing into the depths.

Luna and Iris stood in awe; their hearts were filled with gratitude for the cosmic journey they had experienced. The ocean whispered its thanks and the stars above twinkled in acknowledgment of the newfound harmony.

And so, Luna and Iris carried the song of the celestial whales in their hearts; a song that reminded them of the interconnected dance of all living things and the universal language that binds the cosmos together.

As they left the magical ocean behind, Luna and Iris knew that this celestial melody would forever guide them on their journey, a reminder that in the vast tapestry of existence, every note, every being, has played an essential part.

99

The Quest for Harmony

Luna and Iris embark on a quest to restore harmony to a disrupted realm. They learn about the value of balance and cooperation in maintaining peace.

Once upon a time, in a realm not bound by the rules of our world, Luna and Iris found themselves in a place where harmony was disrupted. The once tranquil land, filled with vibrant colors and melodies, now echoed with discordant notes and chaotic hues.

Curious and concerned, Luna and Iris embarked on a quest to restore balance to this disrupted realm. Their journey led them through enchanted forests, across shimmering lakes, and beyond towering mountains. Along the way, they encountered mystical beings and wise creatures who shared fragments of ancient wisdom.

As Luna and Iris continued on their quest, they learned that harmony wasn't merely the absence of conflict but a delicate dance between contrasting forces. The creatures they met emphasized the importance of balance, like the ebb and flow of tides or the cycles of day and night.

Guided by the lessons of cooperation and understanding, Luna and Iris faced challenges that tested both their individual strengths and their teamwork. They discovered that true harmony arose not from uniformity but from the acceptance and celebration of diversity.

The realm responded to their efforts, gradually transforming from chaos to coherence. Colors became more vibrant, and melodies once again filled the air with a soothing cadence. Luna and Iris witnessed the magic that unfolded when beings, despite their differences, worked together toward a common purpose.

The quest for harmony became a journey of self-discovery for Luna and Iris. They learned that pure balance wasn't an external achievement but an internal alignment of mind, body, and spirit. The enchanted realm, now restored to its former glory, radiated with a beauty that transcended the visual and auditory.

Luna and Iris returned from their quest, carrying with them the restored harmony of the realm and the profound understanding that balance was an ongoing pursuit—one that required constant attention, openness, and a willingness to embrace the ever-changing symphony of life.

100
The Rainbow's End

Luna and Iris follow a rainbow to a magical place where they discover the beauty of diversity and the importance of embracing differences.

Once upon a time, in a world of dreams and possibilities, there lived a curious and adventurous cat named Luna and her friend Iris. Luna was not an ordinary cat—she had a heart that yearned for exploration and a spirit that longed for new experiences.

One day, in a land where colors danced in harmony and the air filled with the sweet scent of diversity, Luna and Iris found themselves at the beginning of a magnificent rainbow. As they gazed upon the vibrant arch stretching across the sky, curiosity twinkled in their eyes.

With a shared glance, they took a step onto the colorful path, and suddenly, the world around them transformed. The ground beneath their feet felt softer, and the air carried melodies of unity. It was a magical place where every hue had a voice, and together, they created a symphony of acceptance.

As Luna and Iris ventured further, they encountered creatures of various shapes, sizes, and colors. Each being possessed a unique brilliance that added to the kaleidoscope of their surroundings. The duo marveled at the beauty that arose from the coexistence of differences.

The first inhabitants they encountered were the Spectrum Butterflies, whose wings sparkled with every shade imaginable. Butterflies, in all their diverse glory, fluttered about in perfect harmony. Luna and Iris learned that each butterfly embraced its colors, contributing to the breathtaking mosaic above.

Moving on, they encountered the Chromatic Chameleons, masters of adaptation. These creatures could change their colors to match their surroundings. What truly impressed Luna and Iris, however, was the chameleons' celebration of their uniqueness. They taught the duo that blending in didn't mean sacrificing individuality.

Luna and Iris discovered the Prism Palace at the heart of the rainbow, a dwelling place for beings from every corner of the spectrum. The inhabitants, known as the Radiant Residents, lived together in peace, appreciating the hues that made them who they were.

In the presence of the Rainbow Sage, an ancient and wise entity, Luna and Iris learned a valuable lesson. The sage explained that true harmony arises not from uniformity but from the celebration of differences. Each color, each being, played a crucial role in the creation of a vibrant and resilient world.

As Luna and Iris bid farewell to the Rainbow's End, they carried with them a newfound understanding. The journey had taught them that diversity was not just a reflection of external appearances, it was a celebration of unique strengths, perspectives, and stories.

Back in their world, Luna and Iris cherished the memory of the rainbow and the lessons it bestowed upon them. They understood that embracing diversity was not only a magical journey but also the key to creating a more colorful and harmonious existence.

About the Author

Gabriella Rujsz is a heart-centered writer and spiritual storyteller whose work is inspired by the quiet miracles of everyday life. The spark for her book was ignited by Luna, her beloved feline companion, whose gentle presence and playful soul opened a portal to something deeper—a reawakening of the inner child and the birth of what she calls the "Master Mechanic" within. Through Luna, she rediscovered innocence, wonder, and a new way of seeing—a shift in perception that changes everything.

Her stories invite readers to soften, to look again, and to see the world not through fear, but through the eyes of peace, love, and gentle curiosity. Her path is devoted to helping others believe in healing, to awaken the forgotten child within, and to nurture a way of seeing that brings light to even the quietest corners of the heart.

With a background in mindfulness, healing, and soulful reflection, her writing offers sanctuary and depth. She reminds us that when we return to wonder, we return to truth—and in that return, we begin to truly see.

Printed and bound by CPI Group (UK) Ltd, Croydon, CR0 4YY
05/05/2026
02102759-0009